Killer Queen
The Hunted

By
Heather McAlendin

E P

Eternal Press
A division of Damnation Books, LLC.
P.O. Box 3931
Santa Rosa, CA 95402-9998
www.eternalpress.biz

Killer Queen: The Hunted
by Heather McAlendin

Digital ISBN: 978-1-61572-383-6
Print ISBN: 978-1-61572-384-3

Cover art by: Dawné Dominique
Edited by: Alison O'Byrne
Copyedited by: Rose Vera Stepney

Copyright 2011 Heather McAlendin

Printed in the United States of America
Worldwide Electronic & Digital Rights
1st North American and UK Print Rights

All rights reserved. No part of this book may be
reproduced, scanned or distributed in any form,
including digital and electronic or mechanical,
including photocopying, recording, or by any
information storage and retrieval system, without
the prior written consent of the Publisher, except for
brief quotes for use in reviews.

This book is a work of fiction. Characters, names,
places and incidents either are the product of the
author's imagination or are used fictitiously, and any
resemblance to any actual persons, living or dead,
events, or locales is entirely coincidental.

*For Scott.
Thank you for believing in my work
and my weird and wonderful mind.*

Chapter One

I struggled against the hands and bonds that immobilized me. I felt paralyzed. There were flashes of light and fangs, so many sharp, white fangs. My flesh was shredded, blood draining from wounds that covered my arms, my legs and my throat.

"No!" I screamed. "Andrew, where are you? Why can't I feel you? Why won't you help me?"

Suddenly, the bonds released and I sprang forward, reaching out in front of me.

Nothing. There was nothing but cool air and the dark.

"A dream?" I panted. "This was all a dream?"

I ran my tongue over my exposed fangs and lips. It was a nervous habit I developed over the last few years. After a moment or two to quiet my mind, I reached out into the inky blackness and felt the darkness revealing the same feelings I had for the last six months: devastating loneliness.

Reaching up the wall, I felt for the light switch. I blinked quickly as the room flooded with flickering, florescent light.

I sat up in bed, alone; my long, silver hair fell like a curtain around my shoulders. I looked around the room at the blacked out windows and the sealed door. It was a barren, impersonal space excepting a small bed, a single pillow and a well-worn comforter I had stolen from a second hand shop not too far from where I was now living.

This was what my life had become. The life of a former Vampire Queen.

I glanced down at a small cooler that fit snugly under my bed. It was full of ice packs and blood bags.

"Marie." I sighed as I remembered our first visit to the blood bank not so many months ago. "If not for you I'd have starved to death."

Marie Saint Martin was a young, former nun with the gift of sight that I turned into a fledgling vampire. Although not without purpose, her human death and rebirth into the Vampire Clans left me unsettled and grieving. She was the kin of Andrew Saint Martin, the human host and consort I had chosen to become the next leader of the vampires and their first King.

I still refused to feed from any human who would not give themselves freely to me. It sickened me the way these new vampires would feed off anyone or anything.

I sat back and carefully lifted the bag of life-giving blood to my lips, revealed my fangs and drank deeply. I closed my eyes and sighed. Before now, my blood taking was an intimate process. I missed Andrew.

Andrew was home, leading the Vampire Clans and taking care of Marie until she became used to her new life as a fledgling.

I had a job to do and I had to keep that in context before I became maudlin and depressed about my past. My past had brought me to this unsettled present.

Hannah was my chosen one; my first blood according to the Vampire Code. In a jealous rage and filled with greed she chose to break the code, break the rules, and break my heart. Hannah stepped away from me and the opportunity to become Queen, to force her way into the human world and create her own half-blood, motley crew of vampires.

As former Queen, I was responsible for bringing her to justice and with that, ending her miserable life. In an odd twist of fate, I missed out on that justice myself but I had to seek out and end the lives of those Hannah had so wrongly created.

The only problem was I had no clue how many were out there or where they were hiding.

Chapter Two

Feeling suitably refreshed at dusk, I came out from my hiding place and wandered the streets seeking anyone who would lead me to Hannah's remaining brood.

Mine was a lonely task and perhaps righteously so. I was amazed at what the modern world deemed a vampire to be. Modern movies portray us as evil doers; monsters who lust after the taste of human blood. In books, we are sexual deviants using blood to bring us to a frenzied orgasm. Humans choose to speak about us in hushed tones, comparing us to Satan or evil incarnate. There is so much fiction and so little truth to any of it.

Although we are ancient and we do indeed sustain our lives with blood, we are not murderers, thieves, or rapists. It was these and many other misconceptions about our race that I had tried to avoid for hundreds of years. It was the main reason the Ancient Ones created the Vampire Code. Within the code, the vampire race could exist with minimal human contact and we could remain, by all human standards, a myth. The code was a safety mechanism. Too much rogue contact between humans and vampires would sully the bloodline and the pure vampire race would no longer exist.

Now I had to rid the world of Hannah's abominations and in doing so, protect the Vampire Clans and humanity before they meshed so closely together that both were in danger of extinction.

Centuries ago, a whole race of ancient vampires called the Toltecs bred themselves into extinction. I dreaded the same thing happening to my people in the twenty-first century.

"Look, it's the Killer Vampire Queen." A hushed, laughing voice mocked me from the shadows.

"No longer Queen," another chided. "She took a human lover and made him King over our beloved."

"Show yourselves." I placed one hand on my thigh where I felt for the bejeweled dagger Queen Akita gave me before leaving my home so many months earlier. The blade was razor sharp and true. I had severed many vampire heads from their lifeless bodies by its machinations. The only true way to kill a vampire was to pierce its heart and remove the head from its body.

"You are all cowards!" I shrieked into the inky darkness. I could hear movement and breathing but I had yet to discover their hiding spot.

"Cowards?" a disembodied voice said. "You allowed a fledgling vampire to murder Hannah. You, who supposedly uphold the Vampire Code to the letter, funny how time changes things."

I stopped and listened, my vampire blood churning with rage. The words and voice were vaguely familiar to me, like an echo in time.

"Drake?" I whispered. "No, it can't be. You are dead, I watched you die."

Once again I heard the familiar, low male voice chuckling.

"Sometimes the eyes, just as the heart, can be deceived," he said.

Father Drake Von Brugel was an Ancient, older even than I or the Ancient Queen Akita. During the Christian crusades, he had been a formidable warrior of the cross. He travelled many continents on the Pope's behalf to bring the sinful to the side of God. Father Drake knew no boundaries when it came to his faith or his merciless discipline and indoctrination of the soulless.

He was a brutal man. My mind flashed back to our first meeting; seemingly a lifetime ago. In fact, it was many lifetimes ago.

I was a warrior maiden on a quest to find adventure. I had been a trained healer and after I found my family brutally murdered by a warring faction, I set out to start a new life and leave my old life behind in the charred ruins of my tiny village.

It was during one of these sojourns that I came upon a dense thicket in the woods. Deep within the thicket was a clearing where I had noticed a gathering of armed men and horses. As silently as I could, I crept up on the group and sat unnoticed in the dense underbrush.

A very tall, well-built man in a long, black frock drew my gaze. His dark eyes glittered like diamonds in the midday sun and his hair was thick and black. He had a long scar on his cheek that ran from just under his left eye to his jaw. Instead of marring his complexion, it added to the authority and masculinity of the man. When he turned to face the group, I noticed the red and white emblem embroidered into his frock. He was a man of God, a priest!

I moved slowly to get out of line of sight when I heard a grunt. A man, thrown from behind the line of men and horses, fell to his knees in front of the towering priest.

"Do you accept the light of Christ in your heart? Do you release the demon within you to follow as his disciple?" Father Drake stared at the hooded man, prostrate before him.

"I have no God and you speak heresy Priest! I have seen what you and others have done in the name of your God."

The man choked as he spoke. I could well imagine his throat was dry from breathing through the roughly sewn sack that covered his head. What had this priest and his followers done?

Suddenly the priest's fist came down on the man's shoulder and knocked him flat into the dirt.

"Quiet evil doer, your serpents tongue holds no power in the eyes of the Almighty!"

"I do not answer to you."

The man let out a low grunt and quickly jumped to his feet. His actions startled the armed men surrounding him. Before anyone could move forward, he had a weapon in his hand, stolen from the warrior standing closest to him.

With one swift movement, the dagger flashed forward and Father Drake sank to his knees with one hand wrapped around the weapon embedded in his stomach.

"You will go to hell bastard dog!" The dying priest groaned. "I am ready to meet my God with a clear conscience."

I remember clapping one hand over my mouth as I watched the blood pump from his gut. Father Drake's men called out to him, then captured and beat to death the offender who murdered him.

"Yes, Silver, all of what you remember is true." Drake said calmly. "I am no more a priest now than you are a Queen."

"How?" I started to speak, only for the ancient priest to interrupt again.

"Same as you my dear, but my life was spared by one of a race of vampires older than God himself!"

Toltecs? No, they were almost extinct by that time and Queen Akita found and spared the life of the last one!

"Carlos?" Drake smirked as he ran one hand through his dark, wavy hair. "He was indeed one of the last of his kind but there was another and *she* is the reason I stand before you today."

She? I questioned silently. I had not heard a whisper of any female Toltecs surviving their extinction.

"Impossible!" I roared. "Quit trying to distract me Drake. You are still a lying, evil snake."

"Oh, but it is true my dear. At any rate, it is due to that fateful meeting that I stand before you today. I know, such a contradiction in terms being a man of God and yet owing my life to the devil."

"Devil." I sniffed loudly in disgust. "You know nothing of my race if you think we are spawns of the devil. Some humans deserve *that* title in a more literal fashion." "Enough nonsense, Drake. Priest or not, you are in my way and I am here for one purpose only; to destroy Hannah's spawn."

Father Drake stood silently and stared at me. His eyes glowed like coals and a growl escaped from deep within his throat. I still could not fathom him being one of my kind.

"I cannot allow you to destroy that which made me who I am. Through my transformation I have gained more power than I ever had or wanted as a human."

Drake's voice whispered deep within my head. *Besides, in this form I have sent many of you soulless demons back to where the Lord Almighty can deal with you!*

I blinked for a moment as I realized he had just spoken with me telepathically. Just how developed a vampire was he?

"So you still consider yourself a priest, Drake?" I asked sourly. "You are what you hate most and yet you still blindly follow a God who cannot and did not help you in your time of need?" My voice dripped with sarcasm as I watched and waited for Drake to move. He did not disappoint me as he steeled himself then lunged forward, trying to grasp me around the neck.

"I have had younger and more powerful vampires try to kill me Drake and I am still here." I mocked. "Let me guess, you figured Hannah would show you where I was and allow you to bury yourself deep within the Clans to do what you wished? Sorry if your plans were ill thought out." It was the last word that spat from my lips as I quickly moved aside, watching as Drake fell to one knee, missing me entirely.

I heard a distinct hiss from his companions, who until that moment remained hidden in the shadows.

"Stay where you are!" Drake shouted as he raised an immense hand, bidding his minions to come no further. "Hannah is gone?" he mused as he raised himself up to his full height and clapped the dust from his hands. "Yes, of course she is. That is when I started hearing them." He smiled as if discovering a hidden cosmic joke.

"Them? What the hell are you going on about Drake? Have you lost your sense of reason as well as your balance?" My voice was dripping with sarcasm as I watched a faint smile play upon his lips.

"You cannot tell me that the all powerful Silver Devries cannot hear them? Hannah's brood is everywhere, my dear. It is a sorrowful song full of lament and regrets and confusion. Now I understand, but..." Drake stopped speaking, closed his eyes, and holding a hand over his chest, he nodded. "Yes, I see it all now."

His dark eyes snapped open and he stared intently at me. Very slowly, I reached for my blade.

"It was not you, was it, my dear Silver? It was a fledgling and of...of Andrew Saint Martin's line? How sweet that is!"

I shook my head and tried to keep my face as unreadable as possible. He, like Andrew had developed his gifts very quickly. Even I did not have such an advanced gift of sight.

"This new breed puzzles you, don't they?" he asked dryly. "It's alright my dear, the new wave of our kind is taking over. You and the Ancients will soon be extinct."

A flood of rage and anguish washed over me. Before I could control the impulse, I sprang forward, fangs bared and my blade aimed at Drake's chest.

Without even so much as a breath or a blink, Drake raised one hand and wiped me aside like nothing more than a butterfly in the wind. He could have snapped me in half if he had a mind too.

I landed with a grunt but quickly leaped to my feet and stood silently, waiting for his next move. Drake drew up to his full height and brushed the dust from his pants, a sly grin spread across his ruggedly handsome face.

"You should be dead now, Silver," he said. "Do not forget that. Now you owe me your life!"

I growled and ran my tongue over the tips of my fangs. "I owe you nothing Drake and once the Clan finds out who and what you are, or at least were, you will have precious few days to gloat."

Once again, Drake smiled and stared directly at me, causing me to shift uncomfortably from side to side. Never had a human or vampire made me so self conscious. I shook off the feeling and lifted my eyes directly up to meet his.

"Do you really presume to think they do not know about me? Do you think Hannah has been the only rogue vampire? The one who turned me may be older than any in the Vampire Clans...older than Carlos."

His deep voice and stare lulled me into a false sense of security. What was happening? My senses dulled and my head felt thick and dense, the vampire blood within boiled and flushed my cheeks and chest.

"What?" I moaned before collapsing to the ground in a heap,

unable to move or feel.

"So much for the all-powerful Vampire Queen." Drake laughed.

Those were the last words I heard before everything went silent and black.

Chapter Three

I woke in the darkness; my head and tongue felt thick as if I had taken drugs. I struggled to move.

"Damn it! " I shrieked. My ankles and wrists were in manacles and my back forced straight against a cold, cement wall.

"Drake!" I yelled in a hoarse, dry-sounding voice. "Drake, where the hell are you and where am I?"

I tried to search out with my mind but even the air around me was lifeless and still. There were no living beings in my presence or within five hundred meters of me on either side.

Squinting, I could barely make out a door at the far end of the windowless room. I panicked...for a moment.

Taking a deep breath, I closed my eyes and quieted my mind.

I am here my love. The smooth, familiar voice soothed my wildly beating heart.

Andrew Saint Martin, my partner, my lover, my friend and willing host for centuries, was the current King of the Vampire Clans. After my misfortune in letting Hannah escape to create her own unholy clan, I and the Ancients chose Andrew as the first male ruler. Hannah had broken the Vampire Code by choosing to infect the true vampire line with second-class human blood. Hannah was my chosen one and each human she chose to bond with, weakened the vampire lineage. For centuries, humans and vampires lived in harmony. Humans blissfully unaware of our existence unless they chose, of their own accord, to become a host and psychically bond with us. As long as a human remained in a vampire's care, they never aged nor required protection. When a human host wanted to be free, the vampire would respect his or her wish and that human would grow old and die, with the memories of service within the Vampire Clans erased for all eternity.

"Andrew." I cried as my body lurched forward, wracked with pain as each manacle bit further into my wrists. "My love; my life, where are you?"

I am always with you love, you know that. Physically I cannot be with you right now but draw strength from my love. Who is Drake Von Brugel? How did he get so much power?

I shook my head, trying to clear the fog I had woken up with.

He is...used to be a priest during the Inquisition. Drake is a brutal man and now a vampire. He has strong psychic powers, not unlike you.

One statement transferred from Andrew's mind to my own.

The Queen of Dreams is awake.

At first, I didn't understand what Andrew was saying. I had never heard of anyone described in that manner in all my years with the Clans.

I shifted, only for the restraints to painfully remind me of my bondage and I let out a low growl. "The Queen of..."

As quickly as Andrew had entered my mind, he was gone. I could feel the imprint of his warm kiss against my cheek. Oh, how I missed him!

My thoughts turned again to Drake and this Queen of Dreams. Could it be?

A sudden burst of light blinded me as the room went from pitch black to daylight instantaneously.

Like a thunderbolt, an image of a willowy, ivory-skinned, raven-haired woman flashed before my eyes, searing her visage into my brain.

"Good day to you, Silver Devries. I understand you and Father Drake are familiar with one another?" A rich, female voice spoke with an as-yet-unfamiliar accent. Her "W" sounded more like a "V" when she talked.

When I opened my eyes, an ethereal looking woman stood before me, dressed in a dark-colored shift. The dress enhanced the pallor of her skin and she seems to glow almost translucent.

"You are quite a sight my dear. Drake, take those awful restraints off the poor creature. She must know by now that there is no way for her to escape." With a flick of her wrist, Drake moved forward to do her bidding. It was as if in he was in a trance. It was unusual, as the Father Drake I had come to know always had cause for a biting, sarcastic remark. What mind game was this vampire "Queen" playing?

The so-called "Queen of Dreams" smiled at me, her fangs luminescent in the bright, white light. *Yes, I do have some influence over Drake, nothing he disagrees with I can assure you.*

She spoke to my mind and her lips remained unmoving. One by one, Drake removed the manacles and stepped back to stand by this female vampire's side.

She raised her hand again and I noticed a distinctive mark on the side of her thin, feminine wrist. The mark was a small tattoo of a bat-like creature with four stars as a crown representing the four corners of the universe. She nodded and smiled again.

"Believe your eyes my darling; I am indeed of the Toltec line. In fact I am the mother creator herself."

"Yaqui!" I stammered, stunned at the awe in my own voice. "But...you don't...you are supposed to be..."

"Extinct?" The ancient vampire mused. "That poor male creature of my race who your Clan saved was not the last of my kind. However, we are dwindling in numbers as we have yet to find a supreme vampire race to mate with. With the fall of the Aztec empire, I had thought for centuries that we had no hope of recovery. With my discovery of Father Drake and the rumblings of a superior male vampire who exists within your own Clan, my heart has hope again."

I rubbed my wrists and shook my ankles to try and increase the flow of blood. I had not fed in almost two days and I was feeling weak, the hunger bubbling beneath the surface.

"I have no idea what you mean by a superior male vampire," I said, trying to hide Andrew's image from my mind.

"Don't be naïve, Silver. After all he belongs to you; you created him." Yaqui licked her swollen, ruby lips as she watched the fascination and then the horror that spread across my face as I finally understood who she was referring to.

"Andrew?" I froze at the thought of this she-devil coming near Andrew let alone the Clan itself. Andrew was my love and my life. I could not allow this to happen, even at the risk of my own demise.

Without a second of hesitation, I gathered what little strength I had and lunged forward, baring my fangs and aiming for Yaqui's throat.

Yaqui shrank back, shrieking for Drake to protect her. Once again, he raised one powerful arm and threw me to the floor like a rag doll. I was furious!

I looked up and noticed the distinctly blank look Drake had on his face. When he first captured me, he was at least in control of his senses. What had this creature done to him?

"Drake." I panted, trying to capture the breath that he had knocked from my lungs. In combination with my thirst, I was becoming weak very quickly, which would not help myself or save Andrew from this Toltec vampire. "Where are your balls, man? You are letting a female control you. What would your men have thought of that?"

Knowingly baiting him, I kept low and waited to see if he'd

strike back or if Yaqui herself would step forward to quiet me.

Much to my amazement neither moved. Very slowly, I stood up and reached for my dagger. Gone! I should have known that they would remove it. Frustration welled up inside me; I began to shake with fury.

"It won't work, Silver." Yaqui purred. "He will do only what I allow him to do and you are too precious a commodity right now to let you die needlessly. I can sense the hunger within you and I will take care of that so you don't wither away or go insane. Not a pleasant way to die. Have you ever watched a vampire starve to death? It is a very painful process indeed."

"I would rather die and go insane than give you any more clues as to where Andrew and the Clans are located." My anger and hunger caused my voice to sound husky and rough. I was so tired and was trying hard to focus. I could not afford to lose my senses...not now.

The Toltec vampire walked forward, holding my gaze with each step. Ensnaring me in the inky blackness of her eyes, I became frozen and unable to move or speak. My thoughts were jumbled and panicked as I watched her lick her moist lips and reveal her extended, glistening fangs. My heart sped up and I could feel the rushing of blood in my ears.

Drake stood just behind her, his arms hung loose at his side. The blank look I had seen earlier was still there but with every movement she made toward me, I noticed a flicker that was not present earlier—or was I imagining things?

"You are so beautiful; and your hair. I can see that you are aptly named, my dear." Yaqui ran one long, slender finger over a lock of my long, silver-colored hair. If I had any will to move, I would have shuddered in repulsion.

Yaqui moved in very close to my face; so close, I could feel her breath on my cheek and neck and she seemed to inhale the very essence of me. Every muscle in my body tensed as her hand drew down my neck to just above my collarbone and hovered there, stroking lightly with her fingertips. I could feel how cool and smooth her skin was as it touched mine. In any other circumstance, it could have been a lover's caress.

My eyes darted sideways at Drake, almost wishing he would wake from his trance-like state.

"Don't worry about the good Father; he will have you in time. Right now, you are mine and I intend to see what is so special about the great Queen! Do you know how long it has been for me? Since I fed from another female vampire...an Ancient such as you?"

She means to kill me! I thought. My brain squirmed at her continued touch, I thought of those lips and teeth slicing a vein and draining any remaining blood I had left. It didn't seem real.

"Oh, I have no plans to kill you my darling. You have to understand how intriguing you are to me. You live amongst humans, couple with humans and bond with them. I am fascinated you have not taken over such a pitiful race. Then again, there are always exceptions to those rules now aren't there?"

Andrew.

"Andrew," she whispered into my ear. "Yes, he is an unusual and powerful creature, comparable to Father Drake."

It seemed as if Yaqui viewed Drake as her possession. My fatigued brain tried to find even the smallest weakness that I could use that to my advantage.

"Although Drake is a strong man and a wonderful companion in many ways, I always wondered what it would be like to have a man after he had succumbed to vampirism, especially one such as Andrew." Yaqui purred as she drew close to my neck and chest and ran her tongue along the length of the vein that pulsed there. I could feel my chest heave and my body shudder in disgust. Yaqui mistook it as misguided sensuality.

The hatred I felt for this creature, this ancient she-devil, was beyond anything I had ever felt for either a human or vampire. My thirst was so overwhelming but my love for Andrew kept my wits intact.

"Your hatred for me will make this all the more sweet, my dear. I will take you when you least expect it. Hatred is akin to love and passion, is it not?" The ancient vampire hissed low into my ear, her breath was warm and moist. "It won't be much longer, I promise you that. I do not want you to die before I drain the last drop of your precious blood myself. Your blood is my salvation."

My eyes and head began to feel very heavy and thick. My eyelids fluttered, but before they closed, I caught sight of Drake. With all of Yaqui's attention on me, it seemed as if her hold on Father Drake had weakened enough for him to come to his senses. His face contorted in an angry, hateful scowl as he watched Yaqui caress and kiss my cheeks and neck.

The last thing I heard before losing consciousness was a familiar male growl as Drake lunged forward and grasped an unwary Yaqui by the throat.

Chapter Four

"Wake up! Get up now if you want to keep your life!" a male voice ordered from above my head.

I opened one eye and squealed as ice-cold water sloshed across my chest and face. The salty, sweet smell of fresh blood flooded my nostrils and my pulse sped up with excitement. My body craved nourishment and like a starving beast, I grasped the flesh that was placed before me and drove my fangs into it, drinking deeply.

The blood was dark and warm, and so delicious. I kept my eyes closed as I continued to suckle, not caring who or what was watching me feast.

As I continued to drain the presented flesh of its blood, I felt warmth slowly seeping back into my limbs; my lips felt plump and my cheeks burned. Finally, after what seemed an eternity, a rough hand grabbed my hair and forced my mouth from the cooling flesh.

"You'll be sick soon if you don't stop."

From deep within my throat, a low growl emanated a warning. When I opened my eyes, I saw Drake standing in front of me, his powerful arms crossed over his chest and his face contorted in a scowl. Streaks of gore and blood streaked his pants and leather boots. The smell of death permeated the air.

I lifted my hand and wiped my mouth of any remaining trace of blood. I was satiated and felt stronger than I had in days.

"What are you looking at, Priest?" I asked sourly.

Drake shook his head in disbelief and pointed one large finger down to my feet.

Yaqui lay in front of me in a bloody, broken heap. Her neck was broken and torn open. I had gorged on her blood. It was no wonder I felt so restored, so powerful! Her blood was the most ancient off all vampires. She was, or at least had been, the head of the Toltec line. Now she lived on in me.

"How ironic," I muttered. As I glanced up, I viewed a wry smile that was spreading very quickly across Drake's face.

The giant man shifted from one foot to the other as he stared down at the lifeless body of the Ancient Vampire Queen. The muscles in his arms and legs rippled as he moved.

"No irony involved in this," he said dryly. "She broke her word to me and that is unacceptable."

I blinked for a moment and stared, incredulous at the thoughts that were building in my brain. He had actually cared about her.

Forgetting that Drake had Ancient blood running through his veins, I was startled when he spoke.

"Yes, even I have a heart. I was lost after she bonded and turned me. She was all I had in the world other than my thirst for power. Yaqui promised me a seat at her right hand after she conquered your Clan. Now I see it was just a veiled attempt to take your blood and your lover. She was so taken with a King...a human turned Vampire King."

"Why did you break my bonds? Why did you feed me? Surely you know now I could end your life?" I asked, almost not wanting to know the answer.

Drake was silent at my question. I steeled myself for a lunge or blow against me.

A long, deep sigh escaped his throat and he laughed quietly at the confused look that must have been spreading across my face.

"You could kill me if you want," he said, "but I think you need me just as much as I need you right now."

His arrogant smugness was irritating but I kept silent.

"Nothing from the great Vampire Queen? No words of anger or hatred? Nothing at all? I am no longer even worth a droll thought?" Drake stood and stared at me with bemused eyes as the sarcasm spewed forth from his lips.

"The only thing I need from you is the whereabouts of Hannah's bastards. I know damn well you are familiar with where they are hiding. I have a task to finish and whether you want to help me willingly or not, is none of my concern." My voice was low and calm. I had not felt this confident in days. Whether it was the Toltec blood coursing through me or hatred...I no longer cared.

I stared at Drake from under my eyelashes and waited for his next move.

Drake's feet were quick and silent as he seemingly materialized at my side. I jumped as he thrust my dagger into my hands. "Here, you may need this if you are to follow where I will lead you." He hissed.

The weight of the dagger was familiar and comforting. I could sense, at least for now, that Drake was not out to harm me. I thrust the weapon into my boot and quickened my pace to keep up with his as he hurried out the door and into the night.

Chapter Five

The evening air was cool and fresh on my face as I sped after the long-legged vampire priest. For a brief second a pain caught in my breast as I thought of the cool evenings I had spent with Andrew. They were evenings when he and I would walk around the gardens and talk of flowers and plants. Evenings when I would feast on his lifeblood in the moonlight, which would inevitably lead us to feast on one another in every sexual act imaginable until we lay sweaty and exhausted in the dew-covered grass. He was my partner in every way possible; both while human and as the Vampire King. My heart and body ached with need and my eyes filled with bloody tears at the great sadness I felt being apart from him.

Drake stopped quickly and held his hand up. I brushed my tears aside and silently moved up behind him.

"What is it?" I whispered.

I looked up and frowned as Drake started down at me with a scowl.

"You need to focus on what is at hand and not on frivolous thoughts of lust or fanciful ideas of love."

I shrank back and shook my head. *What do you know of love anyway?*

"Do not presume to know me Vampire Queen. At any rate, you wanted to know where the brood is holding up. We are here. Can you not hear them?"

All I could hear was silence and the beating of my own heart... and Drake's? I had almost forgotten that the Toltec bloodline would enhance my awareness considerably. I closed my eyes very briefly and could hear breathing. Yet the breathing did not belong to either of us!

Drake froze in front me. His large, dark head cocked to the side and his eyes closed. It was like watching a predator smelling or sensing his prey. For a second I could appreciate the danger Drake was putting himself in for me. He had initially sought out Hannah's brood for himself and now he was helping me to destroy them. It was unfathomable.

"You can thank me later," he said dryly. "Right now, I have

vengeance to execute and you will be useful in helping me in that regard."

Vengeance? Why does he want vengeance?

I did not have time to consider the matter any further when Drake crouched forward and placed a finger upon his lips. I nodded and gathered in close behind.

Someone...no...many were just beyond the shadows, well hidden in the thicket of trees just ahead of where we stood. Although I could feel the fledgling vampires, I had never before been able to hear their thoughts and feel their very breath as I could now. It was a thrilling sensation.

Drake thrust a hand forward, an indication we needed to move forward and quickly. I nodded and followed as stealthily as I could. I was amazed such a big man could move so swiftly and without a whisper of a sound.

The faster I moved, the more the ground seemed almost non-existent beneath my feet. I blinked rapidly while my eyes adjusted to the inky blackness beneath the dense trees.

"They are just ahead of us," Drake whispered. "I have been here many times but now they know she is gone. I do not know how I will be greeted and I cannot guarantee your safety."

"You always have to be a smug bastard, don't you? You have lived so long that you'd think..."

A loud cracking noise curtailed my words and broke the silence of the night. Flocks of startled night birds blanketed the velvety-gray sky just above our heads.

"Damn!" I yelped.

Perturbed at my continued lack of silence, Drake swept me aside like so much dust in the wind. I knew if the brood had not known of our presence, they certainly did now and it was my own stupidity. Would my life as a hunter ever end? When would I ever regain any sense of normality? I had taken so much for granted, never assuming my role as Queen would ever be jeopardy. Now that life was just mist in a dream.

"Normal? Since when has being what humans call the undead normal? You and I will never be *normal*. Not many people would consider a former priest turned vampire normal." Drake hissed menacingly as he lurched forward. Before I realized what he was doing, the head of very young vampire girl rolled on the ground toward my feet. I jumped, the blood splatter barely missing my leather boots. The gore from the brutal decapitation clumped in her unkempt, blonde hair.

"How many more?" I yelped, grabbing my dagger from its hiding place.

"Many. Get ready." Just as Drake spoke, a mass of growling, young and very hungry vampires descended upon us.

"May God damn you to eternal hell!" Drake shouted as he tore heads and limbs with a ferocity I had never experienced even at my most vicious.

The young vampires seemed to pour out of every dark crevice and corner of the underbrush. I did not have any time to catch my breath or even think. All my thoughts and actions were on automatic; pure instinct and preservation kicked in as my dagger hit its mark in many a heart and throat.

Hot, thick blood sprayed everywhere and on everyone within arm's length. In short order, a blanket of mangled, torn limbs and heads lay at our feet. It was a horrific sight, even for one as old as I. The loss of life was incredible, and so shameful to the Vampire Code I held so dear for so long.

The fact that Drake and I had destroyed the entire vampire nest in such a short period of time took me by surprise. I was thankful that the night covered most of what we had done with a dense, gray coat. The morning would reveal our bloody deeds to the human world. We...I had to get away from this place. My heart started to pound and my ears rang.

I fell to my knees as a thick stream of bloody vomit escaped my throat and spewed from my lips onto the ground below me.

I could feel a presence hovering over me as I continued to wretch. "What the hell do you want now, Drake? Haven't you seen enough blood for one day?"

"Get up." He growled.

I looked up expecting to see a fist but instead was surprised to see the giant man's hand extended to grasp mine and help me to my feet. He was covered, head to toe, in dense, pungent vampire blood.

Silently, I accepted his hand and rose up slowly, looking at the wreckage around us. I took a deep breath to settle myself and wiped my dagger clean on my pant leg.

"We did what needed doing. There are more but I think it would be foolish to continue tonight. I need to rest." Drake looked tired and suddenly very old as he shuffled off into the dark forest.

"Where are you going?" I asked.

"We need wood. We need to burn and scatter these bodies so the rest of Hannah's brood cannot reclaim them."

I was startled to hear that he knew the ways of the vampire cleansing ritual. I shook my head and realized that Yaqui would have certainly told him of this. Her kind had chosen this manner so that the undead could not reanimate into something far worse than death could ever be.

Thankfully, only a few reanimated vampires existed and The Clans had strict orders to put the wretched creatures out of their misery. Once the undead reanimated, they craved more than just blood for the sustenance they desired. They needed flesh and they inflicted as much pain as possible on both human and vampire alike in order to get it. Their impaired minds pushed all reason and judgment aside, driven by raw, animal instinct. It was horrible to watch anyone die at the hand of a reanimated vampire. I shuddered at the thought of Hannah's bastards coming back in any form.

Looking down at my clothes, I could see cracks in the rivers of blood that had poured down my chest and pant legs during the slaughter. It was now cracking and flaking with every movement; like old, dried paint.

It wasn't long before Drake had dragged out enough dry, weathered wood to start a large fire. We stacked the bodies like cords of lumber until even faces and body parts were indistinguishable from the burning timber.

I clasped my arms close to my chest in a vain attempt to stop from shivering. My heart ached for the lost souls whose ashes would soon be scattered into the wind.

"You are too sensitive," Drake whispered. I felt his presence behind me and the weight of his large hand as it tenderly grasped my shoulder.

"Somebody has to be." The bitterness in my voice was evident and Drake recoiled as if I had struck him. He quickly withdrew his hand and pulled away.

"I understand you may think me a greedy, self-centered monster but I am not. I have lived many years in anger and misguided faith. With the Toltecs, I thought I had found a place I belonged. I am just as alone as I ever was, except now I'll live forever." The anguish in Drake's voice caught me off guard. In that moment, he seemed more human than he had when I first met him those hundreds of years earlier. He felt loss and sadness and he hurt just as much as anyone. I watched helplessly as he stared intently into the burning mass of vampire corpses.

Go to him my love. Show him he was not misguided in his

actions. He has done us a huge service in destroying a large part of Hannah's fledglings.

I closed my eyes as Andrew's familiar voice filled my brain and the core of my being with an aching need. I missed him so much. I could feel his love but I could also feel a change in him. He took his duties as leader of the Clans very seriously, as he did in his nurturing of Marie. He did not need me as desperately as he once did.

I miss you my love and I am tired. I just want to come home. Warmth and affection greeted my thoughts and then, once again, Andrew was gone from my mind. A brief touch just to remind me he was still there.

I wiped more bloody tears from my cheeks. Life for vampires would never be the same; had not been the same for a long time. Instead of preparing them to move forward, I had kept them sheltered in the past by enforcing the Vampire Code. Even in death, Hannah was still making me pay.

Taking a deep breath, I steeled my nerves and walked up to Drake lightly touching his shoulder with my fingers.

"What is it?" He asked without flinching or even turning to look at me.

"It will be dawn soon. We have accomplished all we are going to for today and I think we both need to clean up and rest. I need to think about where to go or what to do next."

Drake turned slowly and I was surprised to see a slight smile playing upon his burgundy-colored lips as he spoke. "For once you have made sense. I know where we can go if you trust me. Of course, if you'd rather, feel free to scout around on your own for a resting place. Either way we don't have much time; maybe an hour or so."

I looked toward the horizon and saw a hint of burnt orange streaking through the navy blue of the night sky. It was beautiful. Even though it had been hundreds of years since I stood before a sunrise, today would not be the day that changed that.

It is myth that the sun is a destroyer of vampires but we do have a sensitivity to light. Besides, when I chose to expose myself to the sunrise, I want to share that day with my one true love.

"I'll follow you Drake. Don't make me regret it," I said, as I quickly kept pace with his long stride through the dense forest. At that moment, I had no one left to trust and I needed him as much as I hated to admit it.

Chapter Six

With what seemed like seconds to spare before the sun rose in all its fiery glory, Drake led me to a thorny weave of brush and weeds. Where did he intend to hide?

Drake cast an amused sideways glance at me and chuckled deep and low in his throat. "Do you always take appearances at such blatant face value?"

I must have looked like a carp taking its last breath with my mouth open and my eyes round with surprise. As I watched, Drake placed his hand on an unnoticeable but apparently solid section of tangled brush. I could hear a discernible clicking sound and then took a step back as a solid, cement door swung open. Behind the weathered, graying cement was an iron gate that protected a lone stone staircase.

"Amazing!" I exclaimed.

"Save the compliments for a more appropriate time. Come inside before we are noticed in the daylight," Drake said as he placed a large hand on the small of my back and propelled me forward into the dark.

The air was cool and silent after the cement door shut behind us. I took a deep breath and smelled...roses?

Small, dim, modern lights had been placed every five feet or so along the walls of this mausoleum. Although the lighting fixtures were new, I could tell someone had recently upgraded them. Dark patches still colored the walls where I assumed oil lanterns or candles had once flickered. This place existed well before the age of modern technology.

The walls grew damp and the air got colder the farther down the staircase we went. A momentary feeling of dread twisted my guts as I began to wonder why I agreed to follow Drake.

"To survive," he said.

I stopped abruptly as his voice jarred me out of my thoughts. "Damn it! Get out of my head. I don't want you there." My shouts echoed and bounced off of the bare, slick walls.

Surprisingly, Drake stopped and turned to face me, his eyes downcast and shameful. "I apologize. Since inheriting this gift from Yaqui. I forget when I am using it. It has become a part of me and you are right, I have no right to invade your privacy. Please, Silver, come with me."

Extending his hand toward mine, I gingerly accepted his offering of peace and followed him through another open door. This time, the door was ornate, ancient and the decoration looked vaguely familiar. The timber was heavy and looked to be oiled oak. I could faintly smell the remains of ancient resin that must have seeped from the pores when the master originally carved the wood.

What I saw in front of me took my breath away. It was a large, furnished room without windows. A modern gas fireplace added warmth and the sparse light revealed a brocade-covered settee and an overstuffed couch. Stacks of books added to the charm of the room and an oak writing desk with chair sat in the corner. Numerous leather bound diaries sat piled high against the wall. The only thing out of the ordinary was a small metal bar fridge that hummed quietly as I glanced around the room.

"What is this place?" I wondered aloud, forgetting Drake was standing close behind me.

"Welcome to my lair," he answered ominously.

A shiver ran down my spine as I thought of the prospect of being alone in this vampire's domicile.

Drake's face broadened with laughter as he shook his head at my momentary terror. "Please," he said in a soft, disarming voice. "I promise no harm will come to you here; especially from me. We need one another whether you want to admit it or not."

I moved slowly around the room, taking in the feel of the place. I closed my eyes and I could almost see Drake writing his memoirs at the old oak table. I could feel the slow and steady beat of his heart as he relaxed and hid here from the prying eyes of the world.

"Perhaps I seem less of a monster now?" he asked.

"Where can I sleep?" I answered flatly. I was not ready to concede.

"You can avoid the question for now. Behind that door are two rooms. Take your pick. If you are hungry feel free to feed."

Drake pointed to the small silver fridge and turned his back to me. "I have to wash up, I feel incredibly grimy. Do what you will. We will talk in a few hours."

Before I could speak, I watched as Drake turned away and walked through an open door at the farthest end of the room. I assumed it was some kind of bathing area. I let him go in silence.

My hunger got the best of me. It had been hours since I fed

on the Toltec Queen's blood and I could feel my thirst rising. I gingerly reached down and opened the small bar fridge, inside lay multiple bags of cooled, ruby-colored blood.

I sat cross legged in front of the fridge and drank deeply from the first bag I could grab from the shelf. The blood within was cold, yet tasted almost sweet and although I was tired I could not help but feel renewed. It wasn't an ideal feast but, for now, it would do.

After drinking my fill, I closed the fridge and sat quietly in the dimly lit room. I could hear nothing; my mind was quiet, which was an odd sensation for a vampire of any age.

I don't know how long I sat before opening my eyes and stretching my arms and legs out in front of me. I felt as refreshed as if I had slept for days but I stank of dried blood and dirt. *Has Drake finished bathing?* I wondered as I stood up, yawned, and stretched again. I walked quietly toward the door I had witnessed Drake open and enter but I had yet to see or hear him return.

I placed my hand on the door handle, my heart pounding with anticipation. What was behind the door? What would I find?

After taking a deep breath, I slowly opened the door and looked quickly up and down the small hallway.

Silence. I could not hear any movement, no running water not even breathing.

"Drake?" I whispered nervously. "Are you still here? I..."

A sudden, almost indefinable change in the air around me caused me to jump and turn.

"Damn!" I shouted as I ran headlong into the man himself. He stood with his arms crossed; tall, dark and unmoved by either my physical proximity or my shrill voice. His ebony hair was damp and lay in waves around his neck and shoulders. I inhaled the scent of sandalwood that seemed to perfume his freshly washed skin and hair.

I staggered back and quickly tried to compose myself.

"I, I..." I felt like such a fool and could not even finish the sentence. The smell of this man turned vampire was so warm and inviting. I closed my eyes briefly and envisioned Andrew, clean and dripping wet from a shower. My heart and soul ached as I thought of his fair hair, blue eyes and full, luscious lips. It had been so long...

"Did I startle you? I apologize," he said.

I expected to open my eyes and see Drake looking down at me, mocking me with his eyes and smile. His face was serene and serious. Not at all the man I knew and feared so many years before.

"It's alright Drake. It's my fault. I should not have disturbed you. Thank you for…"

My words died as one strong hand reached out and drew me close. I struggled against his chest for a moment then succumbed to the feeling of his arms around me. I missed this closeness with someone, a man, a fellow vampire.

Drake's chest rose and fell quickly with each breath and I could hear a strangled moan from deep within him.

"This desire is so human and yet we as vampires cannot seem to control it." He whispered into my hair.

"It's no different than the blood lust." I answered, knowing full well how different it could become.

"Look at me, Silver." Drake moved me away from him and held me at arm's length. "What do you see? How do you feel?"

For the first time I had to admit that Drake was no different than I was. We both were struggling to find our way through life and disappointments. We were trying to cope with the human world and balance that with the vampire within.

I clasped one of his hands in mine and held it to my chest so he could feel the beating of my heart.

"I have lost as much as you have," I said quietly. "We have both made good and bad choices in our lives for different reasons and now we need to help one another to survive and get our lives back in whatever capacity that may be. I see a man who has had to make hard decisions and I feel a kinship in our mutual sorrow."

"Is sorrow all you feel?" Electricity seemed to run down my arm as Drake stroked my hand and fingers. A burning sensation warmed by belly and thighs as I looked up and stared deeply into his dark, liquid eyes.

I shook my head and looked down at my feet. "No, not just sorrow."

"Come with me. Let's get you cleaned up." Gently pulling on my arm, I allowed him to lead me down the dark hall.

A mixed feeling of relief and disappointment twisted my gut as I followed Drake. Just what was I feeling?

Chapter Seven

My heart raced as we entered a small marble bathing room with a large, claw-footed tub and shower. The air was warm and a bit damp from Drake's earlier bath. The room smelled strongly of sandalwood and roses.

"You fed, now be refreshed, then rest. Hannah's minions can wait a few more hours." Drake said in a firm and gentle voice.

I wanted so much to forget Hannah and her bastard vampires ever existed. I could not forget her nor could I forget what I had given up because of her.

"Hush now." Drake's words filled my head and blocked out any other thoughts or misgivings that were flooding my subconscious. "Relax and let the world pass you by for just this one moment."

Before I could protest, Drake's strong hands stripped me of my bloody clothes, removed my boots and even my undergarments. With one swift movement, he picked me up and lowered me into the warm, scented water that filled the bathtub almost to the brim. If I could ever imagine heaven, this would be it.

I sighed heavily as a heated shower of water soaked my hair and ran down the back of my neck.

Drake handed me a small bottle of shampoo and as I lathered the blood and gore from my hair I could feel the world slip away. I looked up and watched as a smile spread across his face. Then, as if in a dream-like state, he knelt down beside the tub and again used a large silver cup to rinse my hair.

My eyes widened as he placed the cup on the floor and returned to my side. I could not move, did not want to move as he cupped my chin and drew my lips close to his face.

"No words for the rest of the night. No words and no regrets," he whispered as he breathed heavily and finally covered my lips with his own. Unfamiliar lust rose to the surface as the kiss continued.

"Drake, I..."

He nodded knowingly and averted his eyes, as if looking at me would break the spell of the moment.

A sudden surge of desire caught me in its grip and I felt myself hungrily biting and suckling on Drake's lips. Tiny droplets of blood welled to the surface and coated our lips with its familiar, salty-sweet taste.

I watched in fascination as Drake's eyes flew open wide in semi surprise. Had he never tasted blood during sex with a vampire? He must have, Yaqui would not have proceeded any other way.

Drake wrapped one arm around my waist and lifted me effortlessly out of the bath water. With a driven frenzy, he kissed my lips, my cheeks and my breasts as he carried me out of the room and down the hall to where the bedchambers lay.

I kept my eyes closed as I allowed every touch and hungry kiss to overload my senses. As he laid my body to rest on a large, overstuffed mattress, I lifted one finger to my lips and tasted a mixture of our blood. It was the ultimate aphrodisiac.

Drake was naked to the waist and stared at me in wonderment as I suckled my fingers. He was indeed an awesome specimen of maleness within human or vampire form. Before any hesitation overtook me, I reached over with one hand and with my vampire strength, I ripped the britches from his waist to reveal strong, well-muscled legs, a flat stomach, dark, curly pubic hair and a taut, erect penis. I could feel the hunger building within both of us.

Slowly and with care, Drake moved to my bedside and placed one hand on my naked belly, which was rippling with excitement. The contrast of his dark skin against my pale, almost translucent skin was startling and more fodder for our desire. Such complete opposites and yet we shared so much similar history.

"I can see inside you, Silver, and I know what you want. Contrary to popular belief, I am not always a brute. I want this to be mutual." He moaned.

I shuddered at the deep, silky, male sound of his voice. I knew he was not above raping a woman but he wanted me to choose him, to want him in this moment.

My voice sounded strangled as I replied. "I want this. I want you."

He needed nothing more than my affirmation. Drake moved into the bed and swept his hand over every curve and line of my body. My back arched in response and my hips moved upward, begging for a touch; begging his body to connect with mine.

As he stroked my skin, I could feel a sultry heat rising from my thighs to my chest and then finally to my cheeks. I drew back my lips to reveal my fangs. As much as I wanted Drake psychically, I also wanted his blood. For a vampire, bloodletting and the act of intercourse could be a violent but highly pleasurable combination.

"So beautiful." Drake moaned as he kissed each of my breasts in turn, teasing the nipples with his tongue and gently grazing them with his teeth.

I grabbed his head and raised it level with my own. As I kissed him, I drew his tongue deep into my mouth. He tasted warm and almost sweet.

I smiled as Drake's teeth grazed my bottom lip; he drew blood. Lapping voraciously, the kiss turned into a bloody frenzy. Soon, both of our sweat-covered bodies beaded with droplets of ruby blood as sweet as wine to the taste.

The delight I felt at seeing and smelling the blood in conjunction with the ecstasy of each touch and kiss was almost overwhelming. My head began to swim in a dizzy haze of lust and want.

Our bodies danced together in unison; the guttural sounds and sighing heaves of breath was the music to which we danced. Finally, Drake pinned my arms above my hair and thrust himself deep within my core. Each stroke sent my skin and body aflame with sensations.

I opened my eyes wide and thrust my hips upward to match Drake movement for movement. With a final crush of our slick, blood-covered lips, we climaxed together. Our cries of release were loud and animal like as we collapsed in a sweaty heap upon one another.

For a moment, our breathing was the only sound. The room around us was dark and cool and quiet.

"We are indeed vampires," I whispered as I settled into the small of his back. I could smell the drying sweat and blood on his skin.

"One cannot fight what they are, Silver. We must embrace and celebrate it. We must live as what and who we are without shame."

Silently, I thought of how this man seemed to have settled so comfortably into the vampire world. As a human, he always seemed full of fear, angst and hatred for his own kind.

I listened as his breathing slowly changed and we both settled into a dreamless sleep.

Chapter Eight

A white-hot pain seared my brain and my eyes, causing me to literally jump from my slumber and the bed I had shared with Drake. I lifted both hands to my head and rubbed my temples. I was alone.

"Drake?" I whispered into the dark room.

Silence.

I carefully lifted my legs and placed each foot on the cold floor. I could not hear any movement. A slight chill ran up my spine at the thought that something had happened to Drake and if so, what was waiting for me outside the door?

How long was I asleep? I wondered quietly.

After finding my way to the door, I silently opened it just a crack. A dim light entered from the hallway but I still couldn't see Drake anywhere.

"Drake!" I exclaimed. All that returned was a dull echo off the bare basement walls.

I turned and moved across the floor and grabbed a satchel full of clothing laying on the floor at the foot of the bed. I hoisted it across my back and ran as quickly and quietly as I could down the hall until I came back to the bathing room.

In mere moments, I washed and dressed in black leggings, a fitted red t-shirt and black, ballet-type slipper shoes. Functional and comfortable. My leather jacket hung on a hook on the wall. Seemingly, someone, most likely Drake, had taken the time to clean it of the blood and gore that had spattered it earlier. I slipped it over my shoulders and strapped my small dagger to my thigh.

Tense, but refreshed, I carefully made my way back up the hallway to the foot of the staircase and listened carefully.

Why can't I hear anything? It was frustrating that even with my vampire senses I could not hear so much as a thought from anyone, not even any humans. What was going on?

I pulled the dagger from its holster and tentatively began tiptoeing up the staircase. The iron gate at the top of the stairs was open, which indicated to me that Drake or someone else had been in and out very recently.

A quick glance downward revealed the remainder of what

looked like a collected pool of blood and large, telltale footprints leading away from it.

"Only one set of footprints?" I muttered, confused as I gingerly stepped over the burgundy-colored puddle and skulked along the path into the forest.

A hushed voice caused me to pause and hide. I strained to listen. Was it Drake?

"I don't want to hear or see you or any of your followers again. Do you understand? There is enough going on without your interference right now. Yaqui is gone and for good reason. Bide your time and…"

I swallowed hard as I heard Drake's familiar voice end abruptly. He must have sensed I was here and listening to every word. The sound of footfall grew faint as whomever he had been speaking with hurried off into the night.

Glancing up the trail, I straightened up and walked toward the spot I had heard the voices. I needed to confront Drake and find out what was going on.

I stopped a few meters away from where Drake stood with his back to me. He held a long, slender blade in one hand; the other was on his hip as he stared off into the distance. I felt a shudder run through me as I recalled our intimacies only a short time before.

"I know you are there, Silver. How much did you hear?"

"Drake, please tell me what is going on? Who were you talking to and whose blood was that outside the door?" I stood silent while I waited for Drake to face me. He didn't even turn as he answered.

"I can't explain it all right now but you have to trust me. In short order, the Vampire Clans will be more powerful than even you can realize. Once we rid the world of the impure bloodline. As for the blood you saw…" He sighed deeply before continuing. "It was unfortunate for one of Hannah's nosy brood. He took it upon himself to come too close to my home and to you. I've taken care of it. It is nothing for you to worry about. His body is now embers, like the others."

The smell of freshly burned vampire flesh was still wafting in the light evening breeze. I closed my eyes and shook my head sadly.

"So much death," I said quietly. "When will it end?"

Despite his own distraction, I knew Drake could feel my frustration and sadness. He turned and placed a large, warm hand on my shoulder. "Soon. It will end sooner than you realize. Come, I know from that poor unfortunate where the majority of Hannah's brood is still hiding. They had scattered throughout the city since her death but they have mistakenly come together now to try and work out what to do and where to go. Together they will die."

Uplifted by the prospect of finding all of them together, I ignored the nagging voice that was whispering loudly in my head. The voice that was asking who or what Drake was referring to about things ending soon. "One thing at a time," I whispered.

"What?" Drake asked as he grabbed my hand and led me through the dark forest of trees, back toward the city.

"Never mind," I muttered. "We will talk later."

Trust in him my love. Soon it all will reveal itself to you. Andrew's voice once again permeated my brain and my heart. A sudden intense stab of guilt froze me in mid step.

What is there to see? What do you know? My mind sought out answers and reason where there was none. If there was anything I truly believed, it was my love and trust in Andrew, my Vampire King.

Chapter Nine

There was a feeling of familiarity as Drake and I hurried silently up the dark alley. Time seemed to slip past the closer we ventured into the city.

All at once, my knees buckled and drove me to the pavement. An animal-like wail escaped my lips as harsh, guttural sounds invaded my brain.

Drake knelt at my side and held my shoulders, reminding me to breathe. In mere seconds, the pain subsided and I sat, cross legged, exhausted and trembling in the darkness behind a large building.

"What...what was that? What just happened?" My breath came in ragged gasps as I struggled to speak.

Exerting a gentle pressure on my shoulders, Drake helped me to my feet. "I have a hard time believing you have never experienced this before? How long have you existed as a vampire?" he asked.

"I think I know what you are referring to," I replied. "Although I have existed for eons, my powers have never quite been this enhanced. I felt and heard these creatures. Hannah's brood?"

I already knew the answer but Drake affirmed it by nodding his head.

"Here? All of them?" A shiver ran through me. *Could it be as easy as this? Could this all end tonight?* I wondered inwardly.

"Think of it as a new beginning. You...we both have given up so much for others. It is time for reclamation and for life to go forward," Drake said as he helped me to my feet.

I stood and stared at him. It was almost inconceivable to me now that he was once a priest. We now had to work together to end what my error in judgment had caused.

An image of fair-haired Marie, Andrew's distant relative flashed in my mind's eye. She was a former nun who, through circumstance and necessity, I had turned into a fledgling vampire. She, in the end, had served justice on Hannah and killed her.

I now knew why this place was so familiar. Marie had taken me here once, to this blood bank, in order to save my life when my thirst threatened to destroy me. It was here that Hannah had revealed her treacherous plan and her minions to me.

"Perfect isn't it?" Drake asked. His dark eyes glittered like diamonds in the moonlight. I kept forgetting he could read my every thought.

I nodded in agreement and shifted back and forth, tossing my bejeweled dagger from left to right hand. I was restless and I could feel the anticipation making my pulse hurried and my breathing labored.

"Silver, you need to keep your emotions in check. These are creatures; animals and nothing more. They are no longer human and not vampires in the truest sense."

I nodded my head once in agreement with Drake. *Ironic, coming from you.*

If he sensed my sarcasm, he said nothing and motioned for me to move with him to the back doorway of the blood bank. I could also smell fear. The fledglings feared living without Hannah and they feared dying without her as well. They were smarter than I imagined.

Drake smiled down at me and then with a powerful kick, he shattered the door handle and the door itself sprang open with a loud twanging noise and a thud.

We rushed into the darkness, anticipating a hoard of new vampires at our heels.

Nothing.

"Where are they? I've lost touch with them," I whispered, concerned that my mind had gone quiet and blank.

At that moment, Drake's face appeared to go blank and his eyes became devoid of any further expression. His jaw set and he was so still I could not tell if he was even breathing.

"Drake? What is it? Is something wrong?" I asked as quietly as I could but still wanted him to hear me.

He remained that way for only a moment but the time that passed felt like hours. "Damn him!" Drake's voice was hoarse and angry as he spoke. "How could I have been so stupid as to trust him?"

I reached out, grasped Drake's sleeve and drew him close to me. "What the hell is going on Drake? You need to tell me now!"

"You want the truth?" He roared so loudly it caused me to bend backward and seek safety in the wall behind me. As suddenly as his temper appeared, it abated and he wrung his hands in front of his chest. "I'm sorry, Silver. This was not supposed to happen like this. It is not time and now it's a wretched interference with our plans."

I was confused but tried to maintain calm as I straightened up and took a step toward him. "Whose plans Drake? Enough lies or misinformation. I deserve to know what is going on here. Hannah's brood did not just suddenly disappear into thin air! Does this have to do with the person I overheard you chastising earlier?"

I could tell by the change in Drake's posture and body language that I was correct in my assumption. Now I had to press onward and find out who or what we were dealing with.

"Set," he said quietly. "It's Set and his followers who have done this. This was not what I intended, Silver. You must believe me."

"Set!" I shrieked. "How is that even possible?"

Set was a myth within the Vampire Clans. Set's followers were distantly related to the Toltec or Mayan vampire race. They thought themselves superior and wore snake tattoos on their wrists to identify themselves and warn others in the Clans. They were creatures more than vampires who bought and sold Clan secrets to the highest bidder.

The Clans thought that Set himself was long destroyed or dead, or as happened to some of the Ancient vampires, mad with age and hiding in self exile from the general vampire population. Set was once a much feared and lauded Prince rumored to have murdered an ancient fertility God in front of his family. His gall was renowned and despised.

Drake raised his hand in an effort to quiet my rising voice. "Are you insane Drake? Even for you this is unexpected. If, and I mean *if*, Set is indeed alive and even capable of intelligent thought at his advanced age why would he be here? What were you trying to accomplish?"

I could tell Drake was struggling to answer. For the first time, he actually looked uncomfortable.

"Drake," I said. "There is no time to think about what to say or not to say. Out with it so we can get on with finding these hateful abominations."

"He is alive. Yaqui convinced him and his remaining followers to join her in taking over the Vampire Clans. With Yaqui gone, I had hoped, with your help, to convince him to join them rather than conquering. Instead, it seems he's decided to take over control of Hannah's brood."

I tried to make sense of what Drake was telling me. My stomach felt oily and I could feel hot bile rising in my throat.

"How did you possibly presume to think Set could be controlled by anyone? Yaqui could have had some hold on him at one point, as she was an Ancient like him, but now with his age and dementia, control will be impossible. His followers are brutal and dangerous. Hannah's fledglings are young and weak; they will never be able to defend themselves or stop Set from taking them over. They will breed uncontrollably now!" My voice shook with anger and disappointment. I had started to trust Drake and even admittedly developed feelings for him. I betrayed Andrew just as Hannah had betrayed me. What did I have left?

Drake met my eyes and my heart fluttered. In those dark eyes, I saw sadness and regret. "Believe it or not I thought I was doing what was best. My intention was to prevent war. Do you have any idea what could have happened if Yaqui had followed through with her takeover of the Clans?"

I winced at the bloodshed and violence between the vampire factions and the possible dethroning and murder of my beloved Andrew.

"You forget who you are talking to, Drake. I was Queen for eons. Please don't think I am unfamiliar with war." It took all my will to control the anger in my voice.

"I have not forgotten anything, Silver," Drake's gaze was intense as he spoke and I had to turn away in order to compose myself. He was referring to so much more than my former reign as Vampire Queen.

"Where is Set now? Can you feel him at all? Is he close by?" I asked, dreading the answer.

"Right, back to business," he said uncomfortably. "It's hard to tell. You know how well some of the Ancients can hide their minds."

I nodded. "True. It is not a gift I have yet mastered, but with Yaqui's blood inside me, I can tell they are either hiding or have moved very quickly from here. I felt their presence very strongly before now."

"They have gone. I remain."

Drake and I jumped and turned toward the slick-sounding, arrogant voice that spoke from within the shadows. I held my dagger so tight that the hilt bit into the palm of my hand. I could feel Drake tense and clench his own blade as he moved in close to my side.

"Set," we answered in unison.

"Indeed, Ms. Devries, and what a distinct pleasure to see you again, Father Von Brugel. I did not think our paths would cross again quite this quickly."

We watched as Set revealed his hiding place and walked from within the shadowy corridor. He was taller than I imagined and walked with a confident swagger. His auburn-colored haired was cropped close to the scalp and his eyes were as dark as pitch. This was not the appearance of a frail, demented elder. Set was whole and strong and unpredictable.

As I quickly scanned his hands and body for weapons, I heard Drake hiss quietly. "He doesn't require psychical weapons. Keep that in mind."

Set stopped and grinned broadly, revealing a mouth full of needle sharp fangs. "Very good Father...oh, it's just Drake now isn't it? Forgive me, as my mind is not what it used to be. I have been away for much too long."

As he spoke, I felt a warmth spread from the centre of my body to my limbs and then my face. It was as if my brain was on fire. The intense heat lasted for only a moment but it was enough to let me know that Set was in full control in this situation and he could have killed me if he had wanted to do so. He could likely kill us both with nothing more than a thought.

"I find the psychic part of my abilities the most rewarding these days. Although I will say, I have developed a taste for modern human blood. It is so much more nutrient rich than those hateful, dirty creatures I had to depend on in the past. Humans have romanticized our kind for so long that they give themselves almost willingly...almost."

Set's voice was low and menacing but he still had not moved. He seemed content to watch and see if Drake or I would make the first move. I was amazed Drake had kept decidedly silent for this long.

I had enough of the silence and decided to speak. "What have you done with Hannah's fledglings, Set? You have nothing to gain by dealing with them."

"On the contrary," he replied. "They pave the way to the future."

"The future does not include half-bred mongrels. We made a deal." Drake growled as he lunged forward only for Set to throw him back with nothing more than a flick of his wrist. A loud crackling sound filled my ears as Drake's large body hit the staircase. I envisioned cracked ribs and a broken spine. I also knew that it would not keep Drake down or quiet for very long.

"I find it quite ironic for you to be talking about mongrels,

Drake. Silver is the closest thing to a pure blood outside of Yaqui and myself that you have ever come in contact with. You should be bowing before her." Set's voice was calm and steady as he spoke.

"The future," I started, "will be ensured by keeping the vampire line as close to pure as possible. By indiscriminately adding any and all humans, we will all become extinct just as the Toltecs. You of all must realize that!"

The last word barely left my lips before I felt a pair of strong hands on my shoulders and a set of fangs dangerously close to my jugular. Bloody sweat beaded my forehead with the effort to keep control over my instinct to lash out and kill this creature. My life was literally in Set's hands.

"I realize now that you are a disappointment, Silver," he said as spittle flung from his lips and trailed its way down my neck and chest. I cringed, waiting for the deathblow. "Have you spent so long in the security of the Clans that you fail to see what is going on in the world around you? Humans are a failed race at best. They kill, maim and spew hatred at one another for no other reason but financial gain. We could put them out of their misery."

Set's hands tightened to a point where I was certain my clavicle would soon be shattered. "If all the humans are all turned or killed then vampires will die as well. We can't feed on one another for long and without human blood we descend into madness. A leader of your capabilities should worry about his people!" I hissed as he slowly cut off the breath from my throat. I knew it was a desperate effort to save myself or at least hold off long enough until Drake could recover.

Surprisingly, Set drew back and released me. I collapsed in a heap to the floor, but at least I was alive. A quick glance up revealed that something other than my plea was affecting Set's frame of mind.

Set clutched his head and reeled backward. "Not possible, not possible," he muttered. He retreated into the darkness until finally only silence filled the room.

"Drake?" I whispered. "Set is gone, but I don't know for how long. Can you move?"

Silence greeted my concern.

I stood up and cautiously walked toward Drake's body. I kept a hand on my dagger and kept looking back to the shadows. There was no way I was going to be caught unaware again by Set or anyone else.

A low moan indicated that at least Drake was alive. How much time had passed since we entered the building? My thoughts were scattered between concern for Drake and trying to figure out what power had distracted Set long enough to save my life.

Andrew. Drake's voice once again invaded my brain. If not mobile, he was certainly well enough to know my thoughts.

"How?" I asked. "I know Andrew has power that can rival even the Ancients—but to control one such as Set?" I shook my head in disbelief.

I watched with interest as the giant, former priest rose from his injuries as if he had just had a simple slip and fall accident.

"The world as you and I know it is changing. Although Set is insane enough to think humans are the saviors of the Vampire Clans, he does have some basis in reality. As the world becomes more modern we in turn need to modernize what we do and how we do it in order to survive. We can't wait for humans to bond or come to us anymore. There is too much information out there to keep our worlds apart much longer."

His voice was tired and heavy but there was some truth in Drake's words. Was it any wonder Hannah chose to separate herself from me? I was a proponent of the old ways but I could not allow Set to take complete control.

"Andrew is a vampire of the new order. You created him, Silver, you and Queen Akita."

A sudden sadness clutched my chest as I thought of Andrew. How much danger was he in now with Set stalking him and us?

"Give your creation some credit," Drake said plainly. "It is his doing that your throat was not torn from that pretty neck of yours."

Unconsciously, I placed a slender hand on my throat and felt the pulse beating beneath my fingers. Human and vampire life was so fragile and somehow I had to stop Set from possibly destroying it all.

Drake made a final inspection of himself and picked up the blade he had cast aside when he fell. "I am fine, thank you," he said sarcastically. "I am fortunate Set was so distracted by you or I could have been torn apart."

I turned and attempted a smile at his levity. "He let you live for a reason. Are you now ready to tell me details about where the hell he came from and why?"

In one fluid motion, Drake swung the blade and placed in into the holster he had strapped to his side. "It's getting late and we have wasted precious hours while Set disappeared with Hannah's minions. I don't know about you but I am thirsty."

"You are avoiding the question like the plague," I said. "Fine, we will quench your thirst but while we do, you will explain to me what is going on—and I want the whole truth!"

Drake nodded silently as we headed down the staircase to the basement of the blood bank. I could smell the fear left behind by Hannah's fledglings. I also smelled blood, freshly spilled vampire blood. It seemed that Set had to demonstrate his power before Hannah's brood went willingly with him.

As we reached the basement, I stood aghast at the shredded vampire flesh that hung from the walls and the drying, arterial blood that coated the stairs and floor. I hung my head in despair.

"They deserved better than this." I sighed.

"Why?" Drake asked. "Our intention was to kill them and scatter their ashes to the wind. How is this different? They were all going to die."

It was a powerful statement to hear but it was the truth. If not Set, then Drake or I would have killed them.

"I know," I said uneasily. "They're the result of a horrible mistake and a break in the Vampire Code. What Set plans to do with them is abhorrent and we have to stop him. These murders have nothing to do with justice; this was pure evil."

Drake shifted uncomfortably before he responded. "I assume that is how my actions so long ago must have been viewed. Hell, it's the truth. I tortured and killed humans in God's name. Now I am so far from that I can never redeem myself. I had thought that I could convince Set to join the Clans if Andrew was willing. The strength of the Toltecs and the Ancients would mix with modern vampires. We could have been invincible! Now we may be on the verge of a vampire war."

Just the thought of my beloved Clans at war with themselves and bringing humans into the mix was too much to bear. If Andrew and the Clans were not already aware, I had to return and see what we needed to do. This situation had gotten severely out of hand.

Drake turned briskly and opened one of the large, glass coolers that held row upon row of life-giving blood. He tossed me a bag, tore open one of his own and with fangs extended, drank deeply.

I hungrily drove my own fangs into the cooled blood. My eyes rolled back as the delicious elixir ran over my teeth and down my throat. I had not anticipated how thirsty I became in such a short time.

By the time I had finished my blood bag, Drake had started and finished his third.

"Done?" he asked as he wiped a small droplet of blood from the corner of his mouth. I nodded and tossed my bag to the floor.

"It's too late to go back to your hiding place. Any bright ideas on where to hide until dusk?" I asked.

Drake grinned slyly and nodded, a locket of his dark hair dropped down over one eye. He brushed it aside and held out his hand to me. "I have an idea, if you are brave enough to follow?" he exclaimed loudly as if daring me to protest.

"I don't have a choice and you haven't gotten me killed...yet." The thought of once again following Drake into the night was unsettling but it was safer for the two of us to be together than separated while Set was roaming the city. What's your plan?" I asked, almost dreading the answer.

"Well, we can go into old fashioned vampire mode. There is a graveyard nearby here," he said.

"Sacred Heart," I whispered. It was the same graveyard where I met Marie Saint Martin, the runaway nun I had turned into a fledgling vampire. "I know the place, let's get going. We have wasted too much time here already and we can't chance Set regaining his senses and coming back."

Chapter Ten

The graveyard at Sacred Heart sat quietly in the moonlight. Age and neglect had taken its toll on the property. Broken and desecrated tombstones lay in shambles and the once well-manicured lawns were tangled and overgrown with weeds and shrubs. The Church itself, once a thriving parish, lay naked excepting the graffiti that covered the outside walls.

Most humans stayed clear of the place, leaving it to the forest creatures and of course, vampires.

Drake lifted a hand and put a finger to his lips. I raised my eyebrow in question to his demand for silence. Out of the corner of my eye, I noticed something moving deep within the shadows.

I crouched low and slipped my dagger from its holster, at the ready if I felt it was necessary. I watched as Drake quietly made his way toward the shadow. The sky was slowly turning from pitch to royal blue. The rising sun would soon expose us; we had to hide and soon.

A deep, rumbling laughter shook me from my thoughts. "What is it?" I yelled. "What the hell is so damn funny?"

I straightened up and walked over to where Drake stood. He was pointing at the ground and grinning like a Cheshire cat.

Cowering in the shadows was a small, black puppy, not more than a few months old. He had pressed his body tightly against the cold marble of a tombstone. The puppy looked visibly shaken and his dark eyes pleaded for leniency.

I could not but share in the laughter as I gently picked up the dog and placed him back on the path where he ran as fast as his unsteady legs could carry him.

"Hopefully his mother is not too far away," I said gently.

"We have to get moving, Silver."

I nodded in Drake's direction. He led me to a darkened mausoleum. It looked weathered by wind and rain and had most likely been the resting place for a wealthy individual or family. The ornate decoration was very elaborate and very beautiful. Someone had taken a lot of time, effort and expense. Tonight it would be my temporary resting place.

I stamped impatiently as Drake carefully opened the heavy

brass door at the entrance of the mausoleum. In mere moments, the sun would be rising and both of us needed to hide and rest.

With an elaborate sweep of his hand and a deep bend at the waist, Drake bade me enter. "Ladies first," he chided. "Not the most luxurious accommodations but..."

"It's fine," I said, cutting him off. I was not in the mood for pleasantries. I wanted to rest and then get back to Andrew and the Clans. The longer we waited, the more opportunity Set had to complete his wish to take over the Vampire Clans and destroy humanity.

I noticed what may have been a flicker of hurt in Drake's eyes before he moved aside and watched as I carefully entered the mausoleum. I could not afford the drama of emotion right now. I had to apply cold vampire logic and action to this situation. My emotions are what caused the beginning of all of this. I didn't expect Drake to understand that.

"I understand that and so much more," Drake said quietly. Without another word, he moved the large slab covering the tomb and cast aside the remnants of its former inhabitants.

"How Hollywood can we get?" I stated, trying to add a bit of levity to the uncomfortable situation. Never in my wildest dreams did I ever think I'd be slumbering in an old used grave like some sort of ancient Nosferatu.

"Ironic I suppose," Drake replied as he lifted me and watched as I lay down on the cool, hard marble surface. In short order he was lying by my side and had pulled the cover slab as far over us as he could. Even with vampire strength, a full-sized, marble slab was a huge chore to move let alone lift.

I listened to Drake's breathing and felt the heaviness of his body as it pressed against me. I was not used to such close quarters but in an odd way it was comforting that I was not alone. Mindful that at any moment Set could find us and destroy us both, I finally settled into a restless, dreamless sleep.

Chapter Eleven

Dusk came sooner rather than later and I woke, stiff and achy from the hours spent lying in the cold, damp crypt.

Drake's eyes remained closed and his body motionless as I carefully and quietly lifted myself from the tomb and jumped cat-like to the floor. The air was still and the entrance was undisturbed. I felt a bit more at ease knowing no one had spied upon us during our slumber.

When will you wake up? I wondered silently, hoping Drake tuned in to my thoughts. I was impatient and paced the floor over a dozen times before I heard a large yawn and a groan from within the crypt.

"Today I definitely feel my years," Drake said as he sat up and stretch his long arms. "This is definitely not a glamorous or comfortable way to sleep. I much prefer my bed. Have you been awake long?"

"No," I answered after a final pace in front of the entrance. "I just want to get out of here and back home. There is much to do and I doubt Set has just been resting while we have been stuck in here."

"Yes, yes I know. Can you blame me for wanting to delay the inevitable just a few more minutes? I hunger again and I feel the need to feed. We don't have time to go back to the blood bank."

I swallowed the urge to scream. I was hungry as well but we, or at least I, had to concentrate on getting home. Once there, I was sure we could persuade one or two vampires to allow us to borrow their human hosts for a quick feed.

"Can you stave off your hunger long enough to get to Andrew?" I asked quickly. I didn't want to get into an argument and we were wasting time.

"Yes, I suppose I can. We need to leave now or I may not be responsible as to what happens on the road." Drake winced as he spoke and his face was pinched and a bit drawn. The blood bags we had consumed the day before had done very little to satiate his appetite. He needed a willing human host.

After smoothing my hair and the wrinkles from my clothing, I motioned to Drake to follow me out of the tomb. The cemetery was dark and silent. We need to move as quickly as possible and remain undetected until I reached Andrew. In the state of hunger Drake was now in, I could not trust him to make rational decisions.

"It will only take a quarter of an evening's travel before we are deep in Clan Territory," I said as I lead Drake out of Sacred Heart and toward the outskirts of the city. He remained silent but seemingly aware as we rushed down the narrow, dusty back roads.

In short order, I was back in familiar territory. The air smelled sweeter the closer we got to the mark but I was ever aware that at any moment either the remainder of Hannah's minions or Set himself could catch us if we were off our guard.

Admittedly, I was worried about Drake and Andrew's first meeting. The intimacies I shared with Drake had left me feeling guilty yet wondering why Andrew had pushed me subconsciously in this direction. Perhaps he was getting ready to let me go? Had he found another that I was unaware of?

So many unanswered, yet selfish questions when the lifeblood of my beloved Clan was at stake. What had I become?

"Sometimes the past is the past for a reason. Silver, you no longer have control or power over the Clan or Andrew. Concentrate on the now and what you need to accomplish. Concentrate on what you and I need to accomplish."

I thought for a brief moment on what Drake has just said. "Some of that is true. Right now, what you and I need to worry about is getting you fed and us safely to Andrew before Set returns. Enough talk! We are wasting time," I replied forcefully, hoping it would quiet Drake. It did and we hurried together in an uneasy silence.

Time passed, as did the rolling hills and dark shadows. When we finally arrived, I stopped suddenly.

"What the hell?" Drake exclaimed as he crashed into me causing us both to tumble to the ground in a heap. He jumped to his feet and stood above me, glowering. His hair was dark and glistening like a halo against the midnight moon above him. He looked like some kind of dark angel. If I had been in any other frame of mind, I think he would have been broodingly handsome.

"I'm sorry," I said as I leapt up and backward, away from him and his burning eyes. "I need a moment to collect myself. We are here."

"Where?" Drake asked as he turned his head back and forth, squint eyed and trying to find any sign of a building or movement in the night. His skin was now waxy and pale. I could tell he would not be able to hold his senses together if he didn't get fresh blood soon.

"Not quite that obvious in order to survive without direct human contact for so many years. The Clans have lived hidden this way for centuries." I answered sharply. My voice sounded more irritated than I would have liked but I too was hungry and dreading my reunion with Andrew.

I led Drake to a densely wooded area and pointed toward a tight cluster of brush and trees.

"Jump," I said.

A quizzical look came over Drake's face, a look that quickly became amusement as he took a breath and leaped as gracefully as a vampire could over a thirty-six-foot wall of trees. I followed suit but not quite as gracefully as my legs were significantly shorter. It was liberating to feel the power as I glided over the tops of the tree branches and landed in the garden below.

I breathed in deeply as the familiar scent of the midnight blossoms filled my senses. Home.

"I can see why you chose this place, Silver. It's breathtaking!" Drake moved forward into the garden, my garden that I had planted so many years ago. It had been a refuge, my place to think and revel in the moonlight.

The light of the midnight moon outlined Drake's large frame. He sat down on the same bench I had, only months earlier when I had made the decision to leave my home and seek Hannah and her fledgling bastards.

Ruby-colored tears trickled from my eyes and down my cheeks as I got lost in a wave of emotion. A loud thud startled me from my thoughts and I turned just in time to see Drake crash to the ground.

I hurried to his side and with every bit of strength I had, I managed to lift him and drag him to the outer door of the compound. His body was pale and limp, his skin was damp and almost translucent.

I heard a commotion within the compound and was startled as the door opened to see Marie's face staring at me from within the darkness. She was as lovely and delicate as I remembered. No longer dressed in her typical black, she had on a lovely transparent shift of white and her shorn locks had grown long and flowing around her shoulders.

"Silver!" Marie exclaimed, her eyes wide in surprise. "I should have felt you here!"

The young woman flew toward me and wrapped her slender arms around my neck, kissing my face, eyes and cheeks. It was not the greeting I expected. Grateful for the display of affection I returned her embrace and kissed her forehead.

We stayed like that for a moment before reality jolted me back to my senses. I pushed Marie away and pointed to Drake's body, which was laying on the path where I had dropped him.

"So, this is Father Drake?" she asked. "Ironic isn't it? A former nun and former priest, now vampires."

It came as no surprise to me that Marie knew of Drake. Andrew would have shared that information and our past with her.

With more power than I had ever had, Marie walked over to the vampire giant and easily lifted him over her shoulder. "How long since he fed?" she asked plainly.

Once I closed my mouth from the shock of what I had witnessed I shook my head and responded quietly. "It has been a couple of days for a full feed that I am aware of. Same for me but he is much larger than I."

Marie smiled and carried Drake forward. I followed close behind; a feeling of cold dread filled my stomach. I was a stranger in what once was my home.

As we walked inside the large, stone house, my heart lurched. Standing at the base of the staircase near the main hall was Andrew, looking every inch the King of the Vampire Clans.

His long, butter-colored hair was in a smooth, neat ponytail at the nape of his neck. Dressed in dark, pin-striped dress pants and a black silk shirt, he looked lean and powerful. Andrew's cheeks and lips were flushed with color. He had just fed.

He granted me a dazzling smile; for a moment, I was back in time and greeting my lover. However, this was not that time nor was it the place to review what was likely ancient history.

"Silver, you look lovely; tired but lovely as always," Andrew stated as he held out his hand to me. I moved forward slowly as if deciding whether going to him was the best idea.

Please don't hesitate. His eyes pleaded with me but I could tell something had changed. "Drake will be attended to. You need to feed and then we have a lot to discuss. I know why you are here but I am sure you knew that already. Come with me."

Hesitantly, I placed my hand in Andrew's and allowed him to lead me up the staircase to the rooms above. The long fingers and strong hand felt so foreign to me now. It was disturbing yet somehow a relief that Andrew and I both recognized our relationship had changed.

The house itself had not changed. I noticed a few more books here and there; Andrew had always enjoyed literary pursuits. It was not so much the things that had changed but the feeling of the place. A new era had definitely begun and was continuing here.

When we finally arrived at the door outside what I assumed was Andrew's resting place, I pulled back. I felt a presence behind the door, a male presence but I could not determine who it was. An unexpected sense of fear jolted through me like electricity. I knew without a doubt if I entered that room, I'd never leave.

Forcing calm upon myself I attempted to smile at Andrew as he placed his hand on the door handle.

"Not just yet," I said, trying to sound calm as I needed to get a better idea as to who or what was waiting for me. "Let me look at you Andrew, it seems like leadership agrees with you. You look wonderful!"

My former consort grinned broadly and pulled me close to his chest, guiding my head to where his heart beat. "I have you to thank. You have given me the opportunity to see life in a whole new way and with a new sense of purpose."

I could hear his heart beating wild and erratic as he spoke. The voice was the same but there was an uneasiness in his words that I had never heard before. Was he trying to warn me of something?

"Silver, please know how much I loved you," he continued. "Although we shall not rule together now, be strong and retain your sense of purpose."

Pulling my head away, I looked up into his blue eyes and saw tears forming. It was enough to reassure me that something was seriously wrong. As we locked on one another, I mouthed one word to him silently. "Set?"

A slight nod and a blink was my answer. I gathered my strength and pushed myself away from Andrew. With one, swift movement I grasped my dagger and steadied myself for what I was sure would be an onslaught.

"Go, now!" Andrew's voice was low and strangled and he placed one hand on the side of his head in obvious anguish. "I can't do this much longer. It is taking every ounce of mental power I had to stop Set from sensing us here. He means to murder you and Drake and I was to help him. All of this sickens me but he is very powerful, Silver. Go!"

Without another word and resisting the urge to look back,

I jumped backward and turned to scale the stairs. I had to find Drake and leave this place before Andrew completely lost any control and Set unleashed his wrath.

The entrance was empty as I jumped down the final four stairs to the floor below. I closed my eyes and sought out Drake with my mind. I had never perfected this talent but I held on to the hope that it would be enough. It was. Drake's presence was weak but discernible and directly below my feet.

I was familiar with the layout of this place as it had been my own original design. In case of emergency, I had secret passages leading to the basement and escape routes that lead underground and into the city. To my knowledge, no one had ever used them. I rushed to the far side of the staircase and placed my hand on a particular spot. The slight movement was enough to release a panel which revealed a hidden door and stairs to the basement.

As I entered, I heard a loud wail from the top floor of the house. My worst fear had come to true and I knew Set had discovered Andrew, alone in the hallway. Now all I could wish for was that Andrew had the wherewithal to hold Set off as long as possible so we could make our escape.

I am so sorry things had to end this way my love. I hurried down the stairs to the bowels of the house.

As I made my way down a darkened corridor, I could hear a muffled sound coming from the room I used to keep for bloodletting ceremonies. Andrew and I had bonded there in what seemed like a lifetime ago.

With one well-placed heel, I shattered the door in two pieces and made my way inside. There, splayed out on a large bed was Drake with a very young female hovering above him. He had his teeth latched to one breast and was suckling like a babe. The young woman had thrown back her head in what looked like ecstasy.

"Drake! I hate to interrupt but we need to get the hell out of here. It's Set."

I did not have to repeat my words as I watched Drake tear himself away from the nubile young girl. Blood covered her throat and breasts. It tinged Drake's mouth and eyes.

Drake had taken enough blood to render the young girl almost unconscious. "She'll sleep it off," he said sarcastically as he wiped his mouth on a loose bed sheet.

"Nice to hear you are back to yourself again," I said. "We have to leave now. It won't take long for Set to discover where we are. No one here can be trusted anymore. Set has gotten to them all with some kind of psychic hold. Andrew was strong enough to hold them off for awhile but now..." My voice strangled to finish as I thought of Andrew, most likely dead and all because of his love for me.

"You haven't been fed yet?" Drake asked as he hurried to button his shirt and pants.

"Not yet, I'll be alright for a bit. We have to get back to town and hide for now. I just don't know where. Where's Marie?"

"She left after bringing me here. I have not seen or heard from her since. Funny, I don't sense anyone right now. That is highly unusual." The concern on Drake's face was enough to move me forward. I pushed passed him and pointed down the corridor.

"Follow me. Let's see if I can remember how to get out of this place."

We hurried together in the darkness until I found the chamber I had been looking for. The door was marked with an ancient vampire symbol meaning "above," it was my way to remind myself where it led.

The air was musty and damp as I entered the chamber. No one had been here for many years. It was a small glimmer of hope that we may actually be able to escape.

Drake pushed me forward and I landed on my knees in the dust and dirt. "There is movement down the hall if you have a way out, let's get to it!"

This was worse than any nightmare. I was escaping a place that had been my home and refuge for centuries.

Not bothering to dust myself off, I grabbed Drake's shirtsleeve and propelled him forward into a deep tunnel. "Keep bent over, you are tall and this tunnel was not meant as a luxury," I said.

A grunt greeted me as a reply. We moved forward into the darkness. As a precaution, before immersing myself the whole way in, I kicked a few strategic places in the dirt and stonewall, and watched as the entrance filled with rock and clay.

"Impressive," Drake said. "Now I am starting to see why you were Queen for so long. You have the ability to anticipate. Smart."

"To be honest," I began, "I hoped to never have to use these tunnels. This will be the first and the last time for me."

The next few kilometers we spent in silence. It was so dark, even with enhanced vision it was rough to determine each step. Then, my own hunger started to gnaw at me, distracting my thoughts and sense of purpose.

"Drake," I said as I waved my hand in front of me, hoping to attract his attention. "Drake! Stop!"

Concerned, Drake stopped dead in front of me and turned around, his face close to mine. "You need to feed. I am surprised you have lasted this long. Take from me, please."

I blinked, trying to adjust my eyes to inky darkness. Did I really want to feed from Drake again? At this point, I could not afford to argue. If my hunger was not satiated, I would descend into madness and all would be lost.

"Fine," I managed. The strength was draining from me and I could barely speak let alone think. I hungrily brought Drake's wrist up to my mouth. His scent was strong and my mouth watered in anticipation. With my lips drawn back, I drove my extended fangs into the large vein that pulsed just under his skin. A delicious geyser of blood filled my mouth and throat and I swallowed hungrily. With each swallow, I latched on tighter and tighter, suckling as if I had never eaten before today. A warmth spread from the core of my body and radiated outward. Ecstasy!

I was lost in the flood of strength returning to my body. With excitement, I bit down hard.

"Enough!" Drake yelled. "You will kill us both if you gorge yourself. Enough."

The loud, shrill voice felt like the sting of ice water pouring on my skin. The shock brought me back to reality.

"I...I am so sorry," I replied. "I got a bit carried away. Are you alright?" I was worried I had taken too much and then we would both be in danger of weakness.

"I'm fine, Silver, but I think the sooner we get out of here and back to the land above, the better off we will be. We are sitting ducks down here. We are both strong enough for now to make the journey with no further interruptions."

For once, I agreed with Drake without any complaints. With a renewed sense of urgency, we moved forward into the darkness. My desire to get out of this dirt cavern came as a surprise to me. As a vampire, I was used to darkness but it was as if claustrophobia was setting in. I desperately needed fresh air.

"I think we may have company ahead," Drake said. His voice was exceptionally low and quiet. I stopped and strained my ears to hear any sound that may have clued in Drake to any unwelcome visitors.

A barely discernible intake of breath was all the alarm I needed to steel my body against any enemy we may be facing. I could feel Drake's body tense as he crouched low in front of me; not unlike a panther waiting to pounce on its prey.

Even though I could hear breathing, I could not hear or feel any thought. Set had certainly done his best to make certain I was unaware of who or what was head of us.

With my heart pounding, I placed one hand on Drake's large shoulder and we moved together as a unit. Neither one of us wanted anything to catch us unaware.

Suddenly, and without warning, Drake lunged forward and a female voice shouted. I could hear a struggle just ahead of me.

"Damn it, Silver, call off your dog!" The female voice shrieked and then Drake let out a loud grunt. A stream of expletives spewed forth and then silence.

"Marie?" I called out, hesitant that the voice was just a trick played by Set to smoke out my position.

"Yes. Please let this big lug know if he tries to bite into me one more time, I will slit his throat for him just as I did Hannah."

A sense of relief flooded through me. Only three of us knew that the fledgling vampire had murdered Hannah. I could only hope she had escaped Set and was here to help us.

Once again, I heard a loud male grunt. "Drake, it's alright. We can trust her." I said.

"We can trust no one, not even one another truly until Set is gone," was his reply. "As far as I am concerned she is just another pawn in his chess game; vampire or not."

"For God sakes Drake," I said impatiently.

"God has nothing to do with this." Drake's voice had gone sterile and cold. I shuddered as a chill ran down my spine.

"Marie, I am so sorry about Andrew." The emotion caused my voice to sound thick and ragged as I thought of Andrew giving up his life for mine.

A sob escaped Marie's throat as she forced her way past Drake. I felt a pair of slender arms find their way around my waist as Marie buried her head in my shoulder and cried.

"I am so sorry," I said again as I stroked her hair and back.

"As I am for you, Silver. I know no matter what happened over the last few months that you loved him. The Clans will be so lost and Set has taken over the majority of the members, save a few Ancients who had power enough to stave him off. What can we do? How can I help?"

"Does he have Hannah's brood with him?" I asked as I released her. The warmth of her tears seeping though my shirt to leave a wet, bloody imprint on my skin.

"I think so." She sniffed. "They are horrible creatures. They have no knowledge of the Code and they attack and kill humans without thought or mercy."

A large presence moved between the two of us, pressing Marie backward against the damp, dirt wall of the tunnel. "I hate to break up this touching reunion ladies, but we have to get moving and get up topside so we can find a safe place to hide and plan what needs to be done about Set." Drake's voice trailed off as he moved back up the tunnel toward the surface exit. I certainly understood his impatience as we had wasted precious moments.

Wordlessly, Marie and I hurried up the tunnel to the surface, where Drake stood waiting, cross armed and stern. Dirty, and so far alone, the three of us looked like bedraggled underworld dwellers. The stars lit our way down a lonely road that led back toward the center of the city.

"Where are we going?" Marie asked.

"I was hoping you could help us with that," I answered.

Drake stopped and quickly turned to face us, his face was a mask of confusion. "How do you expect this little one to help us? She is barely months old in terms of her abilities."

I was about to speak but thought better of it. I knew Marie would enjoy the opportunity to set Drake straight about his misconceptions.

I stifled a laugh as Marie stood as tall as she could and placed one hand on each of her slight hips. It was quite a sight against Drake's imposing figure. She stared him down for a moment before beginning her reprimand. Her eyes glittered like diamonds in the white light of the moon.

I recalled when we first met. Marie was a nun who had run away from the convent. After discovering she had psychic abilities and doubting her own sanity, she felt her best course of action was to hide away from humanity, until I found her that fateful night in the Sacred Heart Cemetery. Her strength of character and the way she had learned and adapted to vampire life in such a short period was astounding even to me. Drake was not going to like this confrontation.

"Father Von Brugel," Marie began, "for all of your talents and abilities you are extremely limited in your view of the world. I have dealt with enough in the last year to qualify me as an expert on both human and vampire behavior. I can read your every thought, every desire and I know about each and every sin you have committed against the human God and nature. I may be small in stature compared to the likes of you, but I am quick and intelligent and I had the wherewithal to murder Silver's first blood, Hannah, where even she had failed. Do you still doubt my ability to be of help to you?"

Even I shrank back when Marie mentioned Hannah's murder. Drake blinked and his mouth hung open like a fish gasping for its last breath.

Drake bent at the waist in a grand display of respect and penance. "Forgive me," he said. "Trust me when I say I am not mocking you. I am truly sorry. You are correct in that at times I am very quick to judge by appearances. It comes from hundreds of years of programming. I will make more of an effort in the future to listen and observe first. I am impressed that you did not back down from me. It is not what I am used to."

A look of satisfaction and acceptance crossed Marie's face. "Apology accepted, Priest. If you dare follow me, I'll show you where we can hide."

"She is most certainly of Andrew's bloodline," I whispered. I had a feeling that I knew where she would lead us but I kept quiet as Marie took the lead and Drake and I followed behind. The dawn would be breaking soon and we had to rest and plan for our confrontation with Set.

Chapter Twelve

I smiled knowingly as the tall brick warehouse came into view. This is where Marie had been hiding out from the world the first time I had met her. My assumptions about where she was heading were correct.

Just as we ascended the rusty metal stairs to the top floor, the sun made her glorious appearance in the sky. I barely caught a glimpse of its brilliance before Marie ushered us into the darkened storage room. I sighed longingly. "Just once to see a complete sunrise, just once."

No one seemed to notice my lament as the heavy door shut behind us. The small circular window was still the only access to light in the room. A heavy fabric covered it and blocked out most of the sun. Enough light came into the room to reveal that Marie still used this place from time to time. The bedding was in a roll on the cement floor and her small portable cooler still hummed with electricity.

"Please tell me you have blood stored in there?" Drake asked as he sat down, cross legged on the floor.

"Indeed," Marie replied. "I always keep a supply...just in case."

"In case of what?" I asked as I flicked the bedroll open and collapsed on it in a tired heap.

I looked up to see Marie brushing away bloody tears. A flicker of sadness washed across her face, and then it was gone. "The first couple of months in the compound with Andrew were very difficult." She stopped short and took a deep breath. "It was hard enough transitioning from human to vampire and Andrew was wonderful, but with the new power and my psychic abilities I could hear everyone's thoughts. It was overwhelming to the point of painful some days. Then to hear the whispers about me and what I had done to Hannah and the things said about you and Andrew. I came here often to block it all out."

I moved to Marie's side and placed an arm around her shoulder. "Marie, I am so sorry. This is all my fault. I have taken so much from you."

She turned to look into my eyes and smiled graciously. "You have given me so much more. I have...had family. At least now I know where I came from and I fit in here with the vampires so much more than I ever did at the convent."

A loud cough from across the room startled both Marie and I, causing us to turn and see Drake staring back at us.

He slowly rose from the floor and brushed off his clothes. After reaching down and extracting a blood bag from the fridge, he nodded toward the bedding. "You ladies rest for a few hours and I'll keep a watch for anything or anyone unusual. I expect you to do the same once you finish your nap. Set could be anywhere and strike at any time. He needs you, Silver, to convince the rest of the Clan to follow him now that Andrew is dead and I am sure he is none too pleased Marie has escaped."

Fatigue and hunger suddenly overwhelmed me. "I won't argue with you Drake," I said. "Let's all feed and rest for a bit. We can't face Set in the shape we are in."

"Silver." Marie said my name weakly. "I can feel him. I have since he made his presence known. Somehow, I can block him and although I can't get directly into his head, I know when he is close. So far I don't feel him anywhere near us...not yet."

Drake moved in close and held her shoulders so tight that I could see Marie wince in pain. His face was a mask of rage and frustration. "Why the hell did you not reveal this to us before now? I could rip your throat out right now you impertinent, young fledgling..."

With lightening speed, I was at Marie's side. It was enough to startle Drake away from her and I stepped between them, fangs drawn.

"Don't you ever touch her again!" I spat. "How is it with all your great abilities to get into my mind that you didn't read Set better? You brought him here Drake or at the very least facilitated it through Yaqui. Think twice before you decide to cross the line again or you will deal with me. I will be the only Vampire standing."

I felt Marie place a small hand on my arm, pulling me aside. "We are all on edge right now. Please let's rest and gain some clarity."

Drake watched in silence as I followed Marie to the bedding and lay next to her. She curled into the small of my back and we both fell into a restless sleep while Drake watched over us. He reminded me of an avenging angel. Despite all his faults and brutish nature, I trusted him to protect us.

I awoke a few hours later to find Drake pacing back and forth like a caged lion at the zoo. His brow was creased and his face muscles were tense. I didn't need psychic abilities to know something was bothering him.

Making sure I did not wake Marie, I rolled away from her and onto the floor. I stood up slowly and approached Drake very cautiously in case he was in one of his moods.

Drake stopped pacing and grimaced. "I don't understand it," he said. "The little one was right; you were right. I can't feel or hear Set anymore. I've lost my edge against him. It was the only thing that kept him from taking Yaqui from me. What is happening? The silence in my mind is disturbing."

I reached forward and touched his arm, he didn't shrink back as I had expected. Instead, he drew my hand to his chest and held it fast.

"Drake, I..." My voice trailed off as Marie interrupted us with a loud cry. I drew back and rushed to her side as she bolted upright from her sleep.

"Horrible torture. Such an evil creature." Marie mumbled almost incoherently. Her eyes rolled upward as if she was having a seizure.

"Marie!" I shouted as I shook her. "Marie, wake up now. Drake. She's not waking up."

Panic surged through me as I shook her harder, hoping it would jar her awake. Drake gently took her from me, placed a hand on her forehead, and closed his eyes. He drew deep even breaths and mumbled quietly. Finally, he lay her back on the bedding where she trembled and then slowly opened her eyes.

"Thank you," she said weakly. "I feel so cold and hungry."

"What did you do?" I asked Drake as I briskly rubbed Marie's arms and back, trying to warm her. I watched as Drake moved slowly across the room and brought back a blood bag for Marie to feed on. "Well?" I asked again.

Drake shrugged his shoulders. "It's hard to explain and I am not even sure I can, at least not very well. When I bonded with Yaqui, it enhanced everything. Somehow, I can reach out and assist someone when they need it. I can take the pain away, so to speak. Maybe because I can physically handle it, I just don't know. Set had control of Marie for a brief moment. She is strong mentally but I think losing Andrew has had an effect, a crack in her mental abilities that Set was able to momentarily abuse. I will keep my attention on her for any further changes that you may not be able to notice."

"Thank you." It was a weak statement but all I could think of. Marie was my last connection to my lost love and it would destroy me if Set took her as well.

"I'll be fine now, Silver, trust me. Drake has strengthened me and the feed has helped. You need to drink too. I didn't know Set could be...*is* such an evil abomination. He has many fooled many into thinking he is the only way the vampires can survive. His greed and lust for power will destroy us all. There is nothing more dangerous than a crazed Ancient vampire."

Drake had yet to rest so I forced him to lie down while Marie and I cleaned ourselves up as best we could with limited supplies. I managed to drain two bags of blood before I abated my thirst. My heart sank at the thought of Set forcing my beloved Clan to follow him or be tortured.

I had to go back and face him. Somehow, I needed to contact the remaining Ancients and ask for their help.

"Akita!" I said aloud. "Why didn't I think of this before?"

"Ancient Queen Akita was the one who made you her first blood? She made you Queen?" Marie asked.

I nodded in acknowledgment. Queen Akita had gone to rest as many Ancients do once they give up their reign. She made me who and what I was. She believed in me and loved me more than any other I had ever known. I had not recently sought her out but with Marie's help, perhaps she would hear me. We had to try.

"Are you up for a challenge Marie?" I asked.

The young fledgling rubbed her arms and slowly walked toward me with her arms outstretched. "Take my hands, Silver. I know what you want to do. Let's try."

We stood together, joined hand to hand almost as lovers but with much more purpose. I closed my eyes as I sought out to join the mind of the Ancient Queen Akita. Marie's breathing changed from smooth to rapid and shallow as she concentrated on the task at hand. Very slowly, an image began to form. It was seemingly only a shadow within a fine mist but I could feel that both Marie and I were touching the same consciousness.

I felt a more solid presence emerging in my mind. It was beloved Queen Akita and the scent of her enveloped me like an embrace. The Ancient Queen's voice was thin sounding, almost frail.

I am here my love. I know what it is you seek but I am uncertain as to whether I can help you. Set is very powerful and very old. His mind is not whole and he has no moral code. Even for a vampire he is particularly brutal. I know you are empty with

Andrew gone and the Clan is losing itself. You are right to return to your people. Trust your instincts and use Set's weakness against him. You have more support within the Clan than you realize, my love. I am tired and must continue my rest. You are never far from my heart. Trust yourself and those with you now. I love you now and always.

With that, she was gone. Marie and I stood close and were clenching onto one another's hands. My heart and mind were empty and a desperate loneliness overtook me.

"Don't be sad, Silver," Marie said softy as she reached up with one tiny hand and stroked my cheek. "I don't think I have ever felt such love between women before; such a bond."

"Love is love no matter whose heart it fills, Marie. Now what do I do?"

Marie looked thoughtfully at me and smiled. A brilliant smile that gave me a glimmer of hope in the darkness of all my doubts. "Do what she asked of you. You were Queen for hundreds of years for a reason, Silver. Take back your power and own it. It will be the last thing that Set will ever expect."

"She is right you know." Drake interrupted in a sleepy voice. "He will send scouts out to search for us, not expecting us to return to him. Marie and I can shield your mind, Silver. We can help you do this. I feel partially responsible so I want to help, if you will accept my help that is."

A sudden sense of calm and purpose washed over me. I knew what I needed to do and if I had to die to put all these wrongs right, then so be it.

"Alright then," I said brightly. "Let's do this and of course I accept your help, Drake. We all need each other's talents right now. I did not reign over the Vampire Clans for well over two hundred years for nothing. I did learn a thing or two in that time and I did personally design that compound."

Drake jumped to his feet and rushed to my side, lifting me off my feet in a strong embrace. He placed me back on the floor softly, smiled at me, and then turned to Marie. "Shall we do this? We have to get our Queen back to her rightful place and rid the world of the pestilence Set has placed upon it. He must not survive. I will be glad once I can toss his bones into the flames of hell and scatter his ashes to the wind!"

Chapter Thirteen

I should have realized the travel back was easy, too easy in fact. The three of us came upon the compound like bandits in the night. The entire trip was uneventful and we specifically went above ground to face whomever Set sent to try and block our way.

Neither Drake nor Marie gave any indication as to what hid in the dense trees ahead of us. Perhaps because they were so focused on Set himself that they failed to detect a band of his minions hiding in the dark for us.

In a blink of an eye, a dozen fledgling vampires strode toward us, coming out of every corner and shadow with dazzling speed.

"Shit!" I exclaimed, barely having time to jump out of the way of clenched hands and gnashing fangs. Drake exploded like a vampire possessed. He knocked more than one fledgling to the ground with a swift punch to the back of the head. Any that dared get closer to him, he rewarded by tearing open their throats and ripping out their hearts with a flick of his blade.

I drew back my dagger and drove it deep and sure into the chests of several young vampires. The ones that remained were like demons possessed, never retreating. One got close enough to hiss, "Bitch" into my ear as he tried to clamp his fangs into my neck. Marie jumped onto his back and ripped his jugular vein clean from his throat with one hand.

A particularly large vampire male came charging at Drake, lunging high into the air above him with hopes to land on and overpower him long enough to rip the lifeblood from him. Drake had other plans as his blade swung through the air, removing the vampire's head clean from his neck before his feet hit the ground.

Finally, every one of the fledglings lay broken and bleeding in a heap in the ground. None remained alive and to make certain of that fact, we cut the remaining heads of each one cleanly off their bodies.

"Was that it?" I panted. "Set could not have assumed these alone would kill us?"

"If he did, he is certainly insane," Marie replied as she tried in vain to wipe the blood from her hands and face with a corner of her torn, stained, white dress.

"Silver, think about it," Drake said firmly. "This was just a distraction. Something is going on in the compound and we need to hurry to get to the root of it. These are dead. We can burn them later."

We had wasted precious minutes fighting these unfortunate souls while Set was taking control of the Clans. I had to gather up the warrior maiden within and face this monster before any more vampire or human blood spilled.

Cautiously, we approached the compound, emerging from the darkness like dark angels ready for the fight. As I walked inside, I strained to hear any sound or movement.

Silence.

"Courtyard," I whispered. "I think they may be in the courtyard."

Drake raised one eyebrow and looked at me. "How do you know?"

"I don't, not for sure," I relied quietly. "It's just a feeling I have. My gut is burning with it."

My warrior has returned. It was simple statement meant only for me and I smiled as Queen Akita's voice rang in my ear. *Your confidence is restored my love.*

Marie rushed to the back exit, ready for a fight.

"Wait," I said. "We have the element of surprise. If I am to reclaim my throne, I must do it as a Queen would. I want to end this as quickly as you do Marie. Vengeance will be mine, but on my terms and not Set's."

I led both Drake and Marie to what was formally my bedchamber. Everything was just as I left it. I opened the large closet to see all my gowns and ceremonial dresses hanging as I had left them.

I had always hated relying on appearances but tonight I needed to appear as strong and in control as I had ever been.

I told Marie to take her pick of clean clothing. Drake seemed content to just wash his hands and face. Any blood apparent on his dark clothing had long since dried and was not readily visible. As for myself, I washed quickly and dressed in red leather from head to toe. From bustier to boots, I was clad in blood red. With my silver hair in a smooth braid down my back, I was as regal and as ominous looking as I was going to get. I could only hope my heart would be as confident as I looked on the outside.

"Wow, look at you! Welcome back, Queen Silver." Drake whistled and grinned broadly.

"Dressed to impress," Marie said. "You will be hard to miss."

"That's the intention, Marie. Whoever remains loyal to the Clans has to know I am back and ready to take control from Set. I can't allow this monster to do anymore damage. The only option is to kill him. Besides that, I need to ensure that Andrew's death was not for naught."

A small smile resurfaced on my lips as I thought of how valiantly Andrew had died. I missed him and would not let him down.

I turned and looked at both Marie and Drake. "You have both been through a lot," I said quietly. "I don't expect either of you to go any further. This is my fight now."

"Like hell," Drake replied emphatically. "We are all part of the Clans now and it is our duty to stand by our Queen. I have a lot to do penance for. I know Marie feels the same. We will fight by your side tonight and as long as we draw breath."

"Thank you," I said. "No sense in delaying any longer."

We moved quickly and silently back up to the main floor and headed toward the courtyard at the back of the compound. The closer we got, the more feelings of terror flooded through me, but it was not my own fear I was feeling.

"Silver," Marie whispered. "Set knows we are here."

I nodded and glanced upward to see Drake wink at me before we made the last few steps to the large terrace that allowed a full view of the courtyard below. To my amazement, below me stood rows and rows of humans in various states of undress. Fledglings were feeding from them, allowed to bond. It was a mass of undulating bodies but there was no sound, no cries of outrage or fear. It was as if they were all deaf and dumb to what was occurring around them.

I was horrified! I had been hearing this unconscious noise deep within me for some time. So far, they were ignoring our presence and I had not physically seen Set. All three of us were on edge, tense and ready for the inevitable fight.

A quick movement from just beyond my line of sight caught my attention. Show yourself you coward, I thought.

"It's not him," Drake said. "I noticed it too but it's not Set. It's a female vampire. Perhaps a rogue or a scout?"

After an indeterminable period of watching the scene below, I could not see or feel any other presence. I needed to make my own presence known.

"Where is the great leader? Where is Set hiding? Has he left you all to fend for yourselves?" I shouted in a loud and strong voice.

It was an odd sight to see vampire and human alike stop, turn as one body, and stare up at me from below.

"What is wrong with them?" Marie whispered.

It was as I suspected. Set was controlling them, just as a Queen Bee did with her hive. They no longer were capable of individual thought; no will of their own. The situation was incredibly dangerous.

Drake stood behind me. His large frame was a comfort to me as I decided how to play this out. He surveyed the area and placed a hand on my shoulder. "Movement again over to the left," he said. "Shall I investigate further?"

"Nice to see you again."

I jumped back into Drake's chest as Set appeared out of thin air and landed directly in front of me. A low, menacing growl emanated from my throat as I drew my dagger and bared my fangs.

I held my left arm out to stop Marie from charging on the Ancient vampire. So far, he had yet to make any move toward us other than to surprise us with his presence.

The grin that spread from ear to ear proved to me that Set thought all of this was a joke, an amusement to him. He truly did not believe anyone could harm him.

"So you have decided to join me? Rule by my side? How wonderful!" Set spread his arms wide and jumped to the banister, balancing precariously on its edge. Contrary to popular belief, vampires could leap vast distances but none of us has yet learned to fly.

"Do you see, my loves?" He was speaking to the minions below. All of whom had gathered together with their arms raised in the air in some grand, grotesque salute. "I told you that together we will take over the world and become the most powerful Clan to rule the world since the doomed Toltecs."

"You really don't get it do you, Set?" I asked. I was clenching my dagger so tightly in my fist that my nails had begun to draw blood, which flowed in rivulets down my wrist to my forearm. "You are dooming all these to the same fate. Stop this now before you destroy every one of us. By joining all human and vampires together into one master race, there will soon be no food, no blood; and as you well know, we cannot feed on one another for long before we extinguish ourselves. You all must see that." I shouted down to the crowd.

"Blasphemer!" Set screamed. Before he could scream at me again, Drake lurched forward and shoved Set off the banister, only to see him fall to the ground and land on both feet, laughing at the failed attempt to harm him.

"Do you see how powerless they are? The great Queen herself cannot touch me, nor can her weak followers." Set mocked us in a high-pitched voice.

I was livid. My body shook with rage and frustration, both at Set for his arrogance and at Drake for allowing his temper to once again control his actions.

"You must die!" A familiar female voice shouted from the back of the crowd. Was she directing this at me?

Before I could give it further thought, I watched a small band of vampires move quickly throughout the crowd below, striking anyone in their path. Set seemed momentarily stunned into silence.

"Lizette." I shouted. "No!" I finally recognized the brave, petite female vampire and her group of rogue vampires.

Lizette had been a trusted messenger and scribe when I first ruled the Clans. She had warned me of the upset within the Clan once Hannah had escaped the compound and gone about creating her own fledglings, contrary to the Vampire Code.

"For you my Queen!" She shouted as she knocked fledglings one by one to the ground without struggle.

What is Set waiting for? I wondered silently. I could no longer just stand and watch. Both Drake and Marie sensed my impatience and moved in close behind me.

"We move, now!" I screamed as we jumped from the same banister Set had mocked me from only a short time before. A mere second before my leather clad feet hit the ground, the mob in front of us became animated. It was a trap after all!

There was no way of knowing which of the unfortunates were still human and which were in the process of turning into fledgling vampires. Adrenaline took over; voices and movement ran together as I acted with only instinct to guide me. I lost track of time and space and I did not know where Marie or Drake were. I felt a rush of wind as hundreds of Set's minions whirled around me, tearing at my hair and face. Thrusting left and right with my dagger, I had only a second to make sure its aim was true and hit the mark, either heart or neck.

Out of the corner of my eye, I briefly saw who I thought was Drake, swinging his blade and beheading many a young vampire. To see so much Clans' blood spilled left a cold chill running down my spine. This is not how it was supposed to be!

"Damn it, Set. Where the hell are you? How can you stand by and watch all these fledglings die for you?" I raged at no one in particular as I jumped and slashed just to make certain I survived. So far, these young vampires were clumsy and inexperienced. Few had been turned long enough to even realize what they had become.

I felt a sting of pain behind me and I winced as I turned to see what had happened. To my amazement, a fledgling had managed to grab the back of my neck with its newly minted fangs. The scratch was not deep but I did not like the fact I that she had caught me unawares. I realized it could happen in this situation but it angered me. I lashed out, grabbed the young vampire and drove my dagger deep within her chest. As I watched the life ebb out of her, I grew sad and I felt a horrible sense of loss. It was not her fault she became the creature she was and I had to kill her.

A new sense of purpose infused me with energy. I turned back to face the mob and watched with pride as Lizette, Marie and Drake did their best to defend my honor and my return to reign.

Blades flashed and the scent of newly spilled blood filled the air. At any other moment in time, it would have been akin to ecstasy to be surround by so much energy and blood.

"Set!" I called out. "Set, I want you! Show yourself!"

"Your wish is my command my Queen!" Set said smugly as he appeared once again out of thin air. As quickly as he materialized, everyone stopped. The mob stopped, Drake and Marie stopped, Lizette stopped. Time itself froze while Set grabbed me around the waist and held me tight against his hard, lean body. His eyes were wild and dilated as he lowered his lips to my ear and whispered, "Do you comprehend my power yet? Do you see what you are up against? You have fire within you, a fire I want to add to my own. Stay with me and I will share all this with you."

I could barely breathe, let alone move. My mind screamed as Set continued to whisper and touch the outline of my body. The rage within me grew as I thought of how helpless I was at this moment. I had no idea this type of power was even possible, so how could I fight against it? Bloody tears welled up and eventually spilled from my eyes in rivers down my cheeks and neck to my bosom. Set stepped back, licked his lips, and watched as the river of blood grew and spread down my chest. He clapped his hands with glee then stepped in close, unzipping my red leather jacket and exposing my flesh to the night air.

"Such a silly notion to live in harmony with humans when you could control them all. You could relearn to control anyone you wanted; whenever you wanted." Set rambled on about how the Ancients had done us a disservice by allowing our psychic abilities to grow flaccid and impotent over the years.

The Code. We have rules...

"Where have those rules gotten you? You are here right now because those rules are outdated, created by morons who felt they had a higher sense of purpose. Vampires are on this earth to dominate and yet they live in the shadows, hiding their infinite power. It's unfathomable and it makes me embarrassed about where I come from. Do you know I used to be worshiped like a God?"

Trust your instincts and use Set's weakness against him. Akita's words rang in my ears. Set certainly had weaknesses; one was his hunger for power and the other for worship and the need for recognition.

Set looked at me thoughtfully and then his eyes went vacant. He moved in close and licked at the pool of bloody tears that had collected between my breasts. I closed my eyes and took a deep breath.

"Please, Set," I whispered. "Please."

His head came up so fast that he nearly collided with my jaw. He stared at me a moment a sly grin came to his lips. "Please what? You want me to spare your friends? I could care less about them. They will all die eventually anyway."

"Please." I began again. "Please don't stop."

Set looked surprised for a moment and then I saw his ego take over any sense he had left in his Ancient brain. "Silver, Silver, Silver," he said in a voice thick with desire as he raised his hand to caress my waist. "I underestimated you; you are a woman after all. I was starting to wonder. It doesn't surprise me though, I am sure Andrew was more a woman than a man with his long, flaxen hair and effeminate features. I am certain that Drake is just a brute. I used to watch Yaqui and him, you know. Their couplings were anything but graceful or passionate."

I swallowed hard at his mention of Andrew. I wondered silently. *Can I do this? I have to or everyone is lost. I will be lost.*

"The power that emanates from you is like nothing I have ever experienced before," I said softly. My voice shook and I could only hope Set would hear that as pent up desire and not anger or fear.

"Ah yes, power makes the world go around. With power comes awesome responsibility. The responsibility of world power has weighed heavily on me since my re-emergence." Set kept repeating this statement over and over again, distracted as he walked between the rows of immobilized vampires and humans. He stopped at Marie and patted her head as if she were a child or china doll.

"Set," I said once again trying to focus his attention on me. I was afraid that if he got too lost in wherever his demented brain was taking him I would never recover nor would those around me. "Come back to me Set, don't leave me this way."

With lightening speed, Set was behind me with his arms wrapped firmly around my chest and waist. I could feel his hot, acrid breath on the back of my neck. He was touching the spot that he had scratched with his vile tongue. I closed my eyes and willed myself not to shudder or reveal how repulsed I was.

"Delicious, so lovely and delicious. We will make a delightful team my dear. The world has yet to see a pair like you and me," he said.

My stomach was churning and it took every ounce of energy to try and shield my true thoughts as I stood, frozen against Set. Finally, he made his way in front of me and stared at me with demented eyes, leering at my naked chest and the dried blood.

"Now, what shall I do? Can I trust you enough to release you? You are so beautiful and my body yearns for you. I have not been with a woman, vampire or otherwise for so long. Being a god is so lonely. No one understands me, not really. I know you do, though, don't you? You reigned supreme for a time but despite minor dalliances nobody understands...nobody...nobody..." Set's voice trailed off and his gaze clouded over as he spoke.

If I'd had use of my hands, I would have strangled the life out him and enjoyed it. I had to focus hard and draw him back to me.

"Let me release you from your loneliness, Set." I hated lying, even to this poor demented soul, but I was getting frantic. The longer this went on, the harder it would be to release everyone. From Set's actions, I knew his mind was disintegrating. For a vampire that was worse than reanimation.

Once again, Set moved in close and sniffed at my neck and hair. "Your scent is intoxicating, my beautiful Vampire Queen," he whispered as he moved his hand up to undo my braid and let my long silver hair hang free down my back.

Set lovingly caressed my shoulders and my arms. I could sense the desire building within him but would it be enough for him to relax his mental hold on me and the others? I could still feel the dagger clenched in my hand.

"Set, please release me." I begged, as well as I could manage to ever fake begging.

A cry escaped my lips as I felt the blood rush back into my arms and legs. I could move! I looked down to see myself naked to the waist. When I looked toward Set, he was grinning lasciviously and reaching for me. I forced myself not to recoil in disgust.

I allowed him to draw me in close, my naked breasts crushed against his chest. I closed my eyes and as he trailed his tongue down one side of my neck, I drew back my own lips, exposed my fangs and imbedded my teeth deep within his flesh.

Expecting Set to pull back from me, I held on to him with a vice like grip. A low moan escaped his throat as he pulled in closer to me. I drank deeply, then released and thrust my dagger forward. It connected with…nothing?

My eyes opened to find myself standing bare chested and alone. Set was gone.

"Damn you!" I raged loudly only to hear Set's laughter reverberating off the compound walls. I quickly gathered up my leather jacket and pulled it closed as best as I could.

"Not quite as far gone as you had hoped my love," Set's voice was shrill and mocked me from every corner and shadow. Very slowly, the hundreds around me began reanimating. I backed up against one of the garden walls and ducked into the shadows, watching and trying to figure out what to do next.

I stared in horror as the blood lust continued. It was as if nothing had happened! *Where are you, Drake? Marie?* My mind was scattered and I was having trouble concentrating. What had Set done to me? Perhaps it was his blood?

Silver! I could hear Drake's mind seeking out my own but I had lost sight of him. My vision was becoming clouded and my thoughts enclosed in a numbing fog. It was the last thing I remembered before collapsing to the ground in the darkness.

Chapter Fourteen

I woke to find myself paralyzed once again; my hands and arms in bonds once again. "No!" I shrieked. "It's my nightmare come true." Groaning, I struggled against my bonds. This was the second time I had allowed myself to get into an impossible situation. It was as if Set had gotten into my subconscious and had recreated a horrible dream. I felt my chest tighten as I panicked.

Defeat and loss were all I could imagine now. I had failed my people and I had failed myself. Everyone I loved was gone. I reached out and could feel no one.

My head sank down to my chest and I felt as if my legs were about to give out.

"What's wrong? Has the great Vampire Queen and Vampire Hunter succumbed? I am indeed disappointed. I thought you would appreciate what I had learned about you."

I slowly lifted my head and blinked twice, trying to make out the shape in the darkness. The voice belonged to Set but so far I could not see him as me mocked me from the shadows.

"I see my Ancient blood was too much for you." He laughed.

"You are a bastard in the truest sense." I spat. "I hope one day, when you least expect it you will have a chance for redemption and it will be refused."

"Redemption? Funny thing for a vampire to be discussing. We are the damned; there is no hope for us!" Set thundered and raged like a wounded animal.

"Show yourself, you coward!" I shouted. "You can't be afraid of me—or are you? Is that what these bonds are for? To stop me hurting you?" I shook the manacles as best I could. My legs and arms were rigid and frozen but I decided to stop allowing fear to control me. I was angry and if it was the only thing I did, Set would be fully aware of my wrath.

"I'm going to leave now. Please try and think pleasant thoughts. The pangs of hunger should not set in for at least forty eight hours or so. By the third day, you will wish for anything to nourish you. In a week, you will become raging and demented. By the time I have infused the rest of these poor humans with vampire blood, you shall be dead and I will enjoy grinding your bones into dust. Parting is such sweet—"

"Get out!" I shrieked, cutting off Set's words with my own. "You make me sick and my own joy is knowing that in time, you will be destroyed by your own ego."

Set's laughter filled the room and then his voice and his presence disappeared. He left me in the dark and the silence, alone.

Chapter Fifteen

"Silver! Come on now, open your eyes."

Am I dreaming again?

I could hear Lizette's insistent voice calling to me. How long was it since Set left me in this room?

"Silver! My Queen! Please wake up. We don't have much time."

"Not possible." I moaned. "All gone..."

I felt hands unbinding me and I collapsed to the floor. My body felt numb and empty. Lizette hovered above me as I looked up, trying to focus on her image. I opened my mouth to speak and instead had to swallow as a mouthful of warm, life-giving blood gushed down my throat. I coughed and sputtered but was grateful as a familiar heat spread to my stomach and my limbs started to radiate warmth.

"Lizette? Where did you come from? You're alive?" I asked as I lifted my head off the floor and wiped my bloody lips on my sleeve. Lizette's face was beaming as she helped me to my feet. I swayed as I tried to steady myself. She may have been petite but she had strength beyond many men. "How long have I been here?"

Lizette's eyes flickered around the room as if seeking out a presence. "A day or so, but we don't have time for any more questions right now. There is a small band of us gathered outside the city. Those of us who escaped. Many are dead now and many will die soon if we don't stop Set. At least three quarters of the city are now fledglings and it will spread throughout the country side if we don't stop him soon!"

I nodded in understanding and gave Lizette a quick hug. "You saved my life. That is something I will never forget."

Lizette tossed a bag at my feet and turned around to keep an eye on the door. "I brought you some fresh clothes. So far we have time on our side, as well as the fact that Set thinks you are dying, if not dead. We can catch him off guard if we hurry," she said.

"The one thing I have learned is never to think I understand that creature," I replied while I stripped out of my red leathers and dressed in the black stretch pants and sweater Lizette had provided. "I underestimated his mind and I almost died because of it. He is not quite as demented as I first thought and he is even more dangerous."

"We know and before you ask, yes, both Marie and Drake are with us. Drake has been instrumental in shielding us from Set."

I sighed with relief at the knowledge that my friends were with Lizette's band of rogue vampires. "Thank you," I replied. "Thank you very much."

"Are you ready?" she asked.

I nodded as I pulled my boots back on.

"Here," Lizette said as she tossed me a familiar looking weapon.

I held my dagger in my hand, its familiar weight felt comfortable as I clenched it tight within my fist. I looked at Lizette, blinking hard so as not to cry. "How?"

"I returned to the compound to see if anyone was alive after we had escaped. I found this on the ground near the far wall. I knew it was your weapon my Queen. I am pleased I could return it to you."

I looked down at the dagger and back at Lizette. "You will be rewarded once this is all said and done my friend. I owe you a lot."

"You owe me nothing, it my pleasure to serve. Now let's get you back to your people. They need you."

I nodded solemnly and then followed close behind Lizette as she led me out the door. No guards stood watch; no one made noise in the halls above us. Set had truly assumed I was doomed to die. I swore at that moment that it would be his undoing.

We hurried through the familiar halls until we once again came out through the back garden entrance. I stopped as the smell of burned wood and flesh assaulted my nostrils. Piles of burning embers and scorched tree limbs littered the ground.

"Some of us came back to burn the bodies, we had to, some were still half alive and we had to make sure..." Lizette's voice trailed off into a thin whisper.

I knew what she was going to say. At least they had done the poor unfortunates a service by ensuring they took care of their remains. "It's alright Lizette, I understand. Let's leave this place. It's nothing but a reminder of death now. This is no longer my home," I said sadly as we continued out of the garden and down a darkened path toward the city limits.

As we walked, I glanced upward at the midnight sky. The stars were incredibly bright. It was a sight that used to bring be comfort and solace, now I could not even take the time to enjoy their magnificence. Maybe one day soon, but not today.

"Where are we going?" I asked quietly.

Lizette stopped and pointed in a northeast direction. "Are you familiar with an old theater building on the north side?" she asked.

I knew the building she meant. It was almost one hundred years old and had shown old vaudevillian acts and then some of the first talkies and black and white movies. The old Pine Ridge Theater was long since a derelict building. Perfect for vampires as most of the structure was without windows and its facade was in ruins, which kept most humans at bay.

"Are you sure that Set does not know of this place?" I asked.

Lizette nodded. "No guarantees, but for now he seems to be too consumed with world domination. He's left us alone for the last two days but I do not know how much longer that will last. We need your help to draw him back to us. If he is allowed to continue creating fledglings we will soon run out of willing hosts and the thought of starving vampires is just too horrifying," she shuddered noticeably at the thought of half-starved, crazed vampires prowling the countryside.

"I'll be the bait," I said. "As long as Set is destroyed I will do what needs to be done."

Even if it requires the loss of my own life.

The two of us hurried the remainder of the way to the Pine Ridge Theater; seemingly undetected or unnoticed by Set and his half-blood Clan. The theater was dark as we approached, if not for my vampire senses, I would not have noticed the guard Lizette had placed high upon the peaked roof of the building.

Once inside, the rag-tag army of remaining Clan members and a few Ancients revealed themselves. It was less than I had hoped for, but I was glad there were still a few loyal members willing to fight Set for their own continuation as a species.

I was surprised to see a few living humans amongst us. They had chosen to remain bonded to their vampire hosts and were allowing members to take turns feeding only when necessary to remain focused and alive. It was something Andrew would have done if he had chosen to remain human.

I had to catch my breath before the guilt I was again feeling over Andrew's death caught up on me.

"Silver!" I recognized the young, excited voice as Marie. My heart soared as I watched her run through the crowd and wrap her arms around my waist, grateful to see me alive. I was just as grateful to see her and I cried as we embraced. "I am so glad you were not lost to Set. Lizette knew you would survive, even Drake believed."

I raised one eyebrow at the mention of Drake's name. "Where is he?" I asked.

Marie looked up at me with her bright, shining eyes and smiled. "He's out scouting. I think he wants to hunt Set more than you do. He was devastated when you could not be found."

I had to admit to myself that it was not disagreeable to know that Drake was concerned. Right now however, I had to focus on gathering the remainder of the Clan together and defeating Set.

I gently drew Marie into my side and motioned to Lizette to join us as the vampires and humans gathered around us. I took a deep breath and straightened up to my full height before attempting to speak. I had to prepare myself for the fact that no one may want to listen to me or even want me there among them.

"Members of the Clan, I respectfully request your attention." The tension was apparent in my voice as I spoke. "This has been a tenuous time for all of us and in part due to my error in trusting an unworthy first blood. My apologies cannot undo what has been done. We have a common enemy among us and we must unite and put aside old wounds and assumptions to deal with him. Set has threatened our very existence and the existence of humanity. I may no longer deserve to lead you but I will pledge my life to ensure we deal with Set swiftly and according to the Vampire Code. I demand vengeance for the loss of the man I made King and for those of you who have lost members of the Clan and your own families." I stopped for a moment and waited to see if there would be any reaction in response to my speech. Silence greeted me.

"Our symbiotic relationship with humans has served us well until now. What Hannah started and what Set threatens to continue will ensure the extinction of both our civilizations. It has already begun. Can we work together to end this?" I asked.

I shifted nervously and held my breath.

"We will work with you, for now," replied a voice from the back of the room.

"Show yourself!" I demanded.

"You demand nothing from me as I no longer recognize you as my Queen. However, we do indeed have a common enemy in Set. I want to regain our way of life as it was, at least partially. We can discuss loyalties later." A tall, thin, male vampire made his way from the back of the theater. He was one I recognized as an elder among us. He had a scarred face and was once one of the warrior clan of vampires from long ago. He was outspoken as to how modern vampires should conduct and lead themselves but loyal to the code and ethics of vampire life.

"Our loyalties are to one another right now, my friend. I welcome your help." I reached forward my hand and was pleased when the elder vampire grasped it with his own. It was more a show of solidarity as his face revealed nothing but disdain for the vampire monarchy. At this point, I would take what I could get. "Thank you," I repeated. "Thank you."

The vampire released my hand and nodded curtly, then made his way back among the throng. There were hushed whispers but no one came forward in negativity. I was glad for small miracles.

A shout startled me as an explosion shook the floor and walls of the old theater. "Everyone out! He's here! Set has returned! Be ready and kill anyone who gets in your way!"

Drake's voice was strong and loud, a force in itself to be reckoned with. I suddenly felt his familiar warmth behind me as the vampire's and humans scattered out of the theater and into the shadows surrounding it.

"I am pleased to see you again, Silver," he whispered low into my ear. "Let's get you to safety."

"I am here to fight with and for my people, Drake. If I am to die today I want you know that..." Drake's lips against mine silenced my voice. His kiss was hard and fast but enough to let me know the intention.

"Fight we shall, my Queen. Follow me!" Drake grasped my hand as I watched Lizette lead Marie out a side door. I knew she would protect the fledgling. We ended up outside with the stars as our only witness to the fight ahead. Set's minions were already confronting the remaining humans and trying to either kill or feed on them.

"I will not allow another slaughter," I shouted in anger.

"Do I hear a whisper on the wind?" Set's voice mocked me from behind the dust and shadows of the fallen theater.

"I only hear the voice of a coward!" I shrieked. I steeled myself against an attack and Drake took position by my side, fangs bared and weapons drawn.

"A coward does not take over the world," Set replied.

"There will be no world left, Set. Have you learned nothing from the Toltecs?" I asked. I knew the dialogue was pointless but I had to try to draw him out.

"The Toltecs were as insignificant as the humans who remain

here. I survived for this purpose. I am God now!" Before I could move, Marie raced out from within the mob, screaming fiercely.

"There is no God! Even if there was, He would certainly not be you!" She moved with such blinding speed that Set did not seem to be able to focus on what was happening before the fledgling bared down on him and drove her fangs into his neck. From within her dress, we could see a flash of a blade before she thrust it upward into Set's chest. A slick, wet sound punctuated the air as Marie repeatability removed and drove the dagger in a dozen times.

"Marie! No!" I yelled as I lunged toward them. Drake restrained me by the wrist and struggled to break free. "She's only a fledgling!"

"It is done, Silver," Drake replied calmly. "Look."

Set's body turned almost translucent as Marie continued to drain his blood. His heart had burst upon the first strike to his chest. He was dead. Once again, Marie had proven herself. She had accomplished what I could not and saved us all because of it.

I broke free and hurried to Marie's side, tearing her from Set's cooling body. "You can't drink once the heart stops Marie, you'll kill yourself too!"

Marie fell against me, quivering from the effort, the blood and from the rush of adrenaline.

"Silver!" Drake shouted. "It's incredible."

I looked up to see a mass of fledglings quickly stop what they were doing and stare off into the night sky. Looks of confusion and fear spread across their faces as the psychic bond they had with Set was broken and they realized for the first time in days that they were truly alone.

Drake directed the remaining Clan members to herd the confused fledglings into a group until we could decide what to do with them all. The sun would soon rise and as we could not return to the compound or the theater, we needed to get to a place of hiding.

"Sacred Heart," Marie whispered. "We will all be safe there for now."

I gathered Marie up into my arms and carried her to where Drake and Lizette stood, watching as the Clan and fledglings alike traveled cautiously together into the night. I smiled down at Marie who had passed out from exhaustion. "You have done Andrew proud little one."

In the distance, a screaming eagle flew over the tops of the trees, guiding us forward into the dawn.

Chapter Sixteen

It took months to repair what had been so severely broken in just a few days of Set's appearance. We tore down the compound, slowly rebuilding it as neither human nor Vampire wanted any reminders of the blood spilled in that place.

After some convincing, everyone decided to allow the fledglings to stay and become a part of the Clan if they desired, and as long as they pledged to adhere to the Code. Drake and the remaining elders slaughtered those who remained defiant, burning their bodies and scattering their ashes into the wind. They did this to set an example as well as to remind the Clan that the Vampire Code remained law.

I watched over and guided Marie as she recovered. In such a short time, she had served justice on both Hannah and Set. I do not know of any fledgling now or in the past who was ever as strong as she proved herself to be.

Lizette never left her side and there were whispers that they had chosen to bond and become lovers as well as the best of friends. I silently gave my approval, as I knew no one better to protect and stand by Marie than Lizette.

After so many months of upheaval, the Clans were still as united as could be expected but the Ancients had not yet made a decision as to whether they would continue with a monarchy-type rule. If they did, I was not aware of whether they would accept me back as Queen or whether the Ancients would chose another, which was their right.

"Drake..." I sighed as I curled up next to his naked body. We had spent a glorious hour reveling in one another, giving and taking pleasure and blood. Our bonding was unmistakable to any who chose to pay attention. "I have yet to hear anything regarding the ceremony of ascension. The next full moon is due and the Ancients remain silent."

Drake wrapped one large, strong arm around my waist and drew me tight against him as he used his free hand to stroke my long, silver-colored hair. "Trust that they will do what is best. If it is you then you will prove them right and if they chose another, I know you will be gracious. Please know I am by your side forever."

With that said, he kissed me behind my ear and growled low causing a shiver down to the base of my spine.

"Enough of that now!" I chided.

"Never," he said. "I can never get enough of you."

I broke out in peals of laughter. It felt so good to be normal again, as normal as a vampire can get. A loud knock on our bedchamber door broke the moment and brought us back to reality.

"Just a moment," I called out as I grabbed a sheer, flesh-colored wrap and closed it tight around my body. When I opened the door, I saw Lizette standing there with an envelope in her hand.

"I believe you are waiting for this?" Lizette said quietly as she handed me the document. She knew it was the decision made by the Council Clan and the Ancients. I physically shook as I took it from her.

"Thank you, Lizette," I said.

The messenger bowed and nodded, and left the room without another word. I closed the door and turned back to Drake who was sitting up in bed, the sheets draped over his narrow waist and long legs. He smiled and patted the side of the bed. "Come here, or would you rather be alone to read this?" he asked.

I walked over to the bed and sat down next to him. "No, I want you here. This will affect you as well."

I turned the envelope over and over in my hands, trying to will the decision to come forth because I was too afraid to actually read it.

"Shall I?" Drake offered, with his hand extended to take the envelope from me.

"No," I replied quietly. "I have to see for myself."

After one more turn of the envelope, I drew my nail across the top and slit the thin paper sheath open to reveal a small piece of parchment. I slowly drew the document out of the envelope and unfolded it flat, then placed it on my lap.

I read the contents, then placed the parchment back into the envelope, and carefully placed it in the fireplace where it quickly burned to ashes.

Drake looked up at me expectantly as I returned to our bed and wrapped my arms around him.

"It has been decided."

Chapter Seventeen

The Covenant or Ascension Ceremony took place on the evening of the full moon in the newly created compound courtyard. At midnight, the night blossoms would be at their most beautiful and release a scent that was as sweet and as close to scent of blood that nature could provide.

I walked the garden perimeter and recalled my first Covenant Ceremony after Queen Akita had called me to become her first blood.

"I choose you to carry on the blood line of the Ancients," she had said. It was an awesome responsibility and one I had not taken lightly. The vampire world was so different than it had been hundreds of years ago.

"Do I truly fit in here anymore?" I asked myself. I was having doubts but I needed to put them aside so I could put on my best face for this evening and for the remaining members of the Clan.

"You are indeed regal looking this evening," Drake said as joined me in the garden. I had chosen a long burgundy-colored dress with a plunging neckline and flared sleeves while he was dashing, dressed in dark gray, his hair slicked back and his face freshly shaven.

"You smell and look delicious." I purred as I lifted myself up on tiptoes to kiss his cheek. Drake grinned broadly, his fangs gleaming brilliantly in the moonlight.

"Ready for all of this?" he asked.

"I am and then I just want to move forward," I answered.

Before we could discuss anything further, the garden suddenly became a hub of activity as vampires and fledglings alike took their places in a semi circle. I was pleased to see how in such a short time we had all come together in a common goal of survival.

Marie and Lizette joined me at my side. They were lovely in matching red, flowing shifts. Marie's face beamed with love and pride as she took Lizette's hand into her own and brought it to her lips in a very public display of affection.

The air was warm and the moon lent its silver glow to the proceedings. I stepped forward and raised my hand, silencing the crowd that was milling around us.

"We have all survived a great trial and come out stronger and more resilient as a Clan." I called out, trying to sound more in control than I actually felt. "None of us know what the future will hold but we must keep open hearts and minds as we move forward in this modern world where humans and vampires must coexist." I felt Drake's large hand on the small of my back, it was the reassurance I needed to get through the next part of my speech.

"As you are all aware, the Ancient Ones, our elders and conscience for thousands of years have had to make a decision as to the future of how the Vampire Code is enforced and how the rule of this Clan will continue." I had to stop and catch my breath as I felt my throat close with emotion and bloody tears began to well up in my eyes, clouding my vision.

"For now," I began again slowly and with purpose, "the wisdom of the Ancients will remain and we shall be ruled by a Queen once again."

A loud murmur began as individuals started to debate the sense of this decision and I knew many would not and did not approve even though they would live within the Code as the Ancients demanded.

"However—" A hush came over the crowd as I continued to speak. "However, your new Queen and head of the Clans will not be me."

A look of confusion and admittedly some relief came over the faces of many in the crowd. Both, Marie and Lizette turned to look at me. They both had tears in their eyes.

"This is nonsense," Marie said angrily. "They can't hold one mistake in all your years as Queen against you!"

I raised my hand again to try and quiet the crowd. I looked over and smiled at Marie, placing a finger to my lips. "Just listen," I whispered. "Please, listen and promise to adhere to what the Ancients have requested. They see more than I or you will ever know."

"There comes a time when definite change is needed," I said, the confidence returning to my voice as I spoke. "The Ancients, in their wisdom have seen this. It started with Andrew, who although he was only your Vampire King for a brief time, he started the Clans on their journey into the modern world. That shall be continued with the enthusiasm and energy of another from his line."

Stunned silence.

"You all served me well and I beg the same for your new Queen and her consort as they have the blessings of the Ancients."

I watched as the realization of what I was saying was dawning on Marie and Lizette. Marie walked forward and grabbed my hands in shock. "Are you certain? Are you sure this is what they have asked of me? I am still a fledgling here among you." A look of sheer panic overtook Marie as she looked frantically from me to Lizette.

"You are strong little one, " Drake said to her. "We will all be here for you."

"As I said before, the Ancients know and see what we cannot. I agree with their decision and I will be here to guide you through. You will make a wonderful new Queen and I know Andrew would be very proud of you. You have a combination of modern-world experience and the knowledge of the old-world code and ethics. You are fearless and I know the Clan sees that after your actions in these last months. You accomplished what I could not." A bloody tear ran down my cheek as the look of fear faded from Marie's face and look of determination replaced it.

Turning back to the murmuring crowd, I took Marie's hand and raised it high into the air, introducing the Clan to their new Queen.

"Marie Saint Martin," I said strongly. "You are the chosen one to continue the Ancient bloodline and rule within the Vampire Code. The Ancients have blessed you and your consort Lizette and charge you with continued protection of the Clan. I pass the crown to you. Do you accept this responsibility?"

A sudden look of peace came over Marie as she tightly held Lizette's hand and they walked forward to face the Clan together. "I accept and I make the blood oath to rule according to the Vampire Code," she replied.

As was required by ceremony, I unsheathed my ceremonial dagger and dragged its razor sharp blade across my wrist. A thin line of blood appeared as I lifted my wrist to Marie to present myself as a supplicant. She bent forward and suckled briefly as a sign that my Ancient blood and the blood of all those Queens before me was now hers.

I stepped back and made room for Marie and Lizette to move forward in my place. "I humbly remove myself as leader of the Clan and promise to support and adhere to your rule, Queen Marie Saint Martin."

A loud thunder of applause came from the crowd and although their acceptance of her surprised me, I also knew that what the

Ancients wanted, the majority would support. It was now up to Marie to prove or disprove her strength as leader of the Clans.

The celebrations went on deep into the night. I watched in fascination as Marie found herself surrounded by Ancients and fledglings alike. She seemed enthralled with it all but I knew, as she had with everything else, her strength and perceptiveness would shine through. She was what the Clan needed to bring them into the twenty-first century.

Drake was silent through most of it all until he moved in close behind me and wrapped his arms around my waist, drawing me close to him. We stood like that for a while before he kissed the back of my neck and turned me to face him.

"Don't be sad. There is a whole world to discover. We have been drawn to each together again for a purpose," he said.

I looked up, searching Drake's dark eyes, and smiled at the reflection of love I saw there. Never had I thought a former priest and Vampire Queen would mate as one.

"No more being hunted and no more the huntress." I sighed.

"You confronted your destiny and lived to tell the tale," Drake said. "Marie will need you. I need you."

The sun was beginning to rise in the east, creating a perfect palette of orange, pink, and blue. Once again, Drake took my hand and we walked back into the shadows. The battle was over. For now.

About the Author:

Heather McAlendin is a multi published author/photographer living in Toronto, Ontario, Canada.

Information about Heather and her work can be found on her website: http://mcalendin.com.

Killer Queen
by Heather McAlendin

eBook ISBN: 9781770650022
Print ISBN: 9781770650107

Price: $ 5.95
Vampire Thriller
Novel of 30,313 words

A modern vampire thriller brimming with lust, betrayal, greed and vengeance.

Silver Devries is a five hundred year old Vampire Queen who, out of betrayal and vengeance, becomes a Vampire Hunter. She must search for a rogue female vampire who threatens the very existence of the vampire clans. Silver's greatest allies become those who should fear her the most...mortals. Fear, hope and unexpected love are the ties that bind vampire and human together as they fight to save both of their worlds from imminent destruction.

Also from Eternal Press:

The Vampire Queen
by Jodie Pierce

eBook ISBN: 9781615723614
Print ISBN: 9781615723621

Paranormal Vampire
Novella of 24,994 words

A young woman awakes to find out not only is she an important Countess but she is also the very first or 'Ancient One' as she is called by her subjects. Her memories of being a vampire or anyone are gone so she must relearn everything (from spells to flying) from the people around her, but can they be trusted?

She learns her main objective as the old Countess was purifying the vampire race and wishes to continue with that work.

The 'Others', powerful and evil vampires, attempt to use her memory loss to their advantage. They had been trying to entice her to their side for centuries. Struggling to remember her past, battling the 'Others' and coping with her new life keep the Countess busy throughout this spellbinding and thrilling novel. Will she succeed in her goals or will the 'Others' win her over to their side this time around?